I0616971

TALES OF DARING
AND DANGER

MORE WILDSIDE CLASSICS

Dacobra, or The White Priests of Ahriman, by Harris Burland
The Nabob, by Alphonse Daudet
Out of the Wreck, by Captain A. E. Dingle
The Elm-Tree on the Mall, by Anatole France
The Lance of Kanana, by Harry W. French
Amazon Nights, by Arthur O. Friel
Caught in the Net, by Emile Gaboriau
The Gentle Grafter, by O. Henry
Raffles, by E. W. Hornung
Gates of Empire, by Robert E. Howard
Tom Brown's School Days, by Thomas Hughes
The Opium Ship, by H. Bedford Jones
The Miracles of Antichrist, by Selma Lagerlof
Arsène Lupin, by Maurice LeBlanc
A Phantom Lover, by Vernon Lee
The Iron Heel, by Jack London
The Witness for the Defence, by A.E.W. Mason
The Spider Strain and Other Tales, by Johnston McCulley
Tales of Thubway Tham, by Johnston McCulley
The Prince of Graustark, by George McCutcheon
Bull-Dog Drummond, by Cyril McNeile
The Moon Pool, by A. Merritt
The Red House Mystery, by A. A. Milne
Blix, by Frank Norris
Wings over Tomorrow, by Philip Francis Nowlan
The Devil's Paw, by E. Phillips Oppenheim
Satan's Daughter and Other Tales, by E. Hoffmann Price
The Insidious Dr. Fu Manchu, by Sax Rohmer
Mauprat, by George Sand
The Slayer and Other Tales, by H. de Vere Stacpoole
Penrod (Gordon Grant Illustrated Edition), by Booth Tarkington
The Gilded Age, by Mark Twain
The Blockade Runners, by Jules Verne
The Gadfly, by E.L. Voynich

Please see www.wildsidepress.com for a complete list!

TALES OF DARING AND DANGER

G. A. HENTY

WILDSIDE PRESS

TALES OF DARING AND DANGER

This edition published 2005 by Wildside Press, LLC.
www.wildsidepress.com

CONTENTS

BEARS AND DACOITS

A TALE OF THE GHAUTS

CHAPTER I.

A merry party merry party were sitting in the verandah of one of the largest and handsomest bungalows of Poonah. It belonged to Colonel Hastings, colonel of a native regiment stationed there, and at present, in virtue of seniority, commanding a brigade. Tiffin was on, and three or four officers and four ladies had taken their seats in the comfortable cane lounging chairs which form the invariable furniture of the verandah of a well-ordered bungalow. Permission had been duly asked, and granted by Mrs. Hastings, and the cheroots had just begun to draw, when Miss Hastings, a niece of the colonel, who had only arrived the previous week from England, said, —

"Uncle, I am quite disappointed. Mrs. Lyons showed me the bear she has got tied up in their compound, and it is the most wretched little thing, not bigger than Rover, papa's retriever, and it's full-grown. I thought bears were great fierce creatures, and this poor little thing seemed so restless and unhappy that I thought it quite a shame not to let it go."

Colonel Hastings smiled rather grimly.

"And yet, small and insignificant as that bear is, my dear, it is a question whether he is not as dangerous an animal to meddle with as a man-eating tiger."

"What, that wretched little bear, Uncle?"

"Yes, that wretched little bear. Any experienced sportsman will tell you that hunting those little bears is as dangerous a sport as tiger-hunting on foot, to say nothing of tiger-hunting from an elephant's back, in which there is scarcely any danger whatever. I can speak feelingly about it, for my career was pretty nearly brought to an end by a bear, just after I entered the army, some thirty years ago, at a spot within a few miles from here. I have got the scars on my shoulder and arm still."

"Oh, do tell me all about it," Miss Hastings said; and the request being seconded by the rest of the party, none of whom, with the exception of Mrs. Hastings, had ever heard the story before — for the colonel was somewhat chary of relating this special experience — he waited till they had all drawn up their chairs as close as possible, and then giving two or three vigorous puffs at his cheroot, began as follows: —

"Thirty years ago, in 1855, things were not so settled in the Deccan as they are now. There was no idea of insurrection on a large scale, but we were going through one of those outbreaks of Dacoity, which have several times proved so troublesome. Bands of marauders kept the country in confusion, pouring down on a village, now carrying off three or four of the Bombay money-lenders, who were then, as now, the curse of the country; sometimes making an onslaught upon a body of traders; and occasionally venturing to attack small detachments of troops or isolated parties of police. They were not very formidable, but they were very troublesome, and most difficult to catch, for the peasantry regarded them as patriots, and aided and shielded them in every way. The headquarters of these gangs of Dacoits were the Ghauts. In the thick bush and deep valleys and gorges there they could always take refuge, while sometimes the more daring chiefs converted these detached peaks and masses of rock, numbers of which you can see as you come up the Ghaut by railway, into almost impregnable fortresses. Many of these masses of rock rise as sheer up from the hillside as walls of masonry, and look at a short distance like ruined castles. Some are absolutely inaccessible; others can only be scaled by experienced climbers; and, although possible for the natives with their bare feet, are impracticable to European troops. Many of these rock fortresses were at various times the headquarters of famous Dacoit leaders, and unless the summits happened to be commanded from some higher ground within gunshot range they were all but impregnable except by starvation. When driven to bay, these fellows would fight well.

"Well, about the time I joined, the Dacoits were unusually troublesome; the police had a hard time of it, and almost lived in the saddle, and the cavalry were constantly called up to help them, while detachments of infantry from the station were under canvas at several places along the top of the Ghauts to cut the bands off from their strongholds, and to aid, if necessary, in turning them out of their rock fortresses. The natives in the valleys at the foot of the Ghauts, who have always been a semi-independent race, ready to rob whenever they saw a chance, were great friends with the Dacoits, and supplied them with provisions whenever the hunt on the Deccan was too hot for them to make raids in that direction.

"This is a long introduction, you will say, and does not seem to have much to do with bears; but it is really necessary, as you will see. I had joined about six months when three companies of the regiment were ordered to relieve a wing of the 15th, who had been under canvas at a village some four miles to the north of the point where the line crosses the top of the Ghauts. There were three white officers, and little enough to do, except when a party was sent off to assist the police. We had one or two brushes with the Dacoits, but I was not out on either occasion. However, there was plenty of shooting, and a good many pigs about, so we had very good fun. Of course, as a raw hand, I was very hot for it, and as the others had both passed the enthusiastic age, except for pig-sticking and big game, I could always get away. I was supposed not to go far from camp, because, in the first place, I might be wanted; and, in the second, because of the Dacoits; and Norworthy, who was in command, used to impress upon me that I ought not to go beyond the sound of a bugle. Of course we both knew that if I intended to get any sport I must go further afoot than this; but I merely used to say 'All right, sir, I will keep an ear to the camp,' and he on his part never considered it necessary to ask where the game which appeared on the table came from. But in point of fact, I never went very far, and my servant always had instructions which way to send for me if I was wanted; while as to the Dacoits I did not believe in their having the impudence to come in broad daylight within a mile or two of our camp. I did not often go down the face of the Ghauts. The shooting was good, and there were plenty of bears in those days, but it needed a long day for such an expedition, and in view of the Dacoits who might be scattered about, was not the sort of thing to be undertaken except with a strong party. Norworthy had not given any precise orders about it, but I must admit that he said one day: —

"'Of course you won't be fool enough to think of going down the Ghauts, Hastings?' But I did not look at that as equivalent to a direct order — whatever I should do now," the colonel put in, on seeing a furtive smile on the faces of his male listeners.

"However, I never meant to go down, though I used to stand on the edge and look longingly down into the bush and fancy I saw bears moving about in scores. But I don't think I should have gone into their country if they had not come into mine. One day the fellow who always carried my spare gun or flask, and who was a sort of shekarry in a small way, told me he had heard that a farmer, whose house stood near the edge of the Ghauts, some two miles away, had been seriously annoyed by his fruit and corn being stolen by bears.

"'I'll go and have a look at the place tomorrow,' I said, 'there is no parade, and I can start early. You may as well tell the mess cook to put up a basket with some tiffin and a bottle of claret, and get a boy to carry it over.'

"'The bears not come in day,' Rahman said.

"'Of course not,' I replied; 'still I may like to find out which way they come. Just do as you are told.'

"The next morning, at seven o'clock, I was at the farmer's spoken of, and there was no mistake as to the bears. A patch of Indian corn had been ruined by them, and two dogs had been killed. The native was in a terrible state of rage and alarm. He said that on moonlight nights he had seen eight of them, and they came and sniffed around the door of the cottage.

"'Why don't you fire through the window at them?' I asked scornfully, for I had seen a score of tame bears in captivity, and, like you, Mary, was inclined to despise them, though there was far less excuse for me; for I had heard stories which should have convinced me that, small as he is, the Indian bear is not a beast to be attacked with impunity. Upon walking to the edge of the Ghauts there was no difficulty in discovering the route by which the bears came up to the farm. For a mile to the right and left the ground fell away as if cut with a knife, leaving a precipice of over a hundred feet sheer down; but close by where I was standing was the head of a watercourse, which in time had gradually worn a sort of cleft in the wall, up or down which it was not difficult to make one's way. Further down this little gorge widened out and became a deep ravine, and further still a wide valley, where it opened upon the flats far below us. About half a mile down where the ravine was deepest and darkest was a thick clump of trees and jungle.

"'That's where the bears are?' I asked Rahman. He nodded. It seemed no distance. I could get down and back in time for tiffin, and perhaps bag a couple of bears. For a young sportsman the temptation was great. 'How long would it take us to go down and have a shot or two at them?'

"'No good go down. Master come here at night, shoot bears when they come up.'

"I had thought of that; but, in the first place, it did not seem much sport to shoot the beasts from cover when they were quietly eating, and, in the next place, I knew that Norworthy could not, even if he were willing, give me leave to go out of camp at night. I waited, hesitating for a few minutes, and then I said to myself, 'It is of no use waiting. I could go down and get a bear and be back again while I am thinking of it;' then to Rahman, 'No, come along; we will have a look through that wood anyhow.'

"Rahman evidently did not like it.

"'Not easy find bear, sahib. He very cunning.'

"'Well, very likely we sha'n't find them,' I said, 'but we can try anyhow. Bring that bottle with you; the tiffin basket can wait here till we come back.' In another five minutes I had begun to climb down the watercourse — the shekarry following me. I took the double-barrelled rifle and handed him the shotgun, having first dropped a bullet down each barrel over the charge. The ravine was steep, but there were bushes to hold on by, and although it was hot work and took a good deal longer than I expected, we at last got down to the place which I had fixed upon as likely to be the bears' home.

"'Sahib, climb up top,' Rahman said; 'come down through wood; no good fire at bear when he above.'

"I had heard that before; but I was hot, the sun was pouring down, there was not a breath of wind, and it looked a long way up to the top of the wood.

"'Give me the claret. It would take too long to search the wood regularly. We will sit down here for a bit, and if we can see anything moving up in the wood, well and good; if not, we will come back again another day with some beaters and dogs.' So saying, I sat down with my back against a rock, at a spot where I could look up among the trees for a long way through a natural vista. I had a drink of claret, and then I sat and watched till gradually I dropped off to sleep. I don't know how long I slept, but it was some time, and I woke up with a sudden start. Rahman, who had, I fancy, been asleep too, also started up.

"The noise which had aroused us was made by a rolling stone striking a rock; and looking up I saw some fifty yards away, not in the wood, but on the rocky hillside on our side of the ravine, a bear standing, as though unconscious of our presence, snuffing the air. As was natural, I seized my rifle, cocked it, and took aim, unheeding a cry of 'No, no, sahib,' from Rahman. However, I was not going to miss such a chance as this, and I let fly. The beast had been standing sideways to me, and as I saw him fall I felt sure I had hit him in the heart. I gave a shout of triumph, and was about to climb up, when, from behind the rock on which the bear had stood, appeared another growling fiercely; on seeing me, it at once prepared to come down. Stupidly, being taken by surprise, and being new at it, I fired at once at its head. The bear gave a spring, and then — it seemed instantaneous — down it came at me. Whether it rolled down, or slipped down, or ran down, I don't know, but it came almost as if it had jumped straight at me.

"'My gun, Rahman,' I shouted, holding out my hand. There was no answer. I glanced round, and found that the scoundrel had bolted. I had time, and only just time, to take a step backwards, and to club my rifle, when the brute was upon me. I got one fair blow at the side of its head, a blow that would have smashed the skull of any civilized beast into pieces, and which did fortunately break the brute's jaw; then in an instant he was upon me, and I was fighting for life. My hunting knife was out, and with my left hand I had the beast by the throat; while with my right I tried to drive my knife into its ribs. My bullet had gone through his chest. The impetus of his charge had knocked me over, and we rolled on the ground, he tearing with his claws at my shoulder and arm, I stabbing and struggling, my great effort being to keep my knees up so as to protect my body with them from his hind claws. After the first blow with his paw, which laid my shoulder open, I do not think I felt any special pain whatever. There was a strange faint sensation, and my whole energy seemed centered in the two ideas — to strike and to keep my knees up. I knew that I was getting faint, but I was dimly conscious that his efforts, too, were relaxing. His weight on me seemed to increase enormously, and the last idea that flashed across me was that it was a drawn fight.

"The next idea of which I was conscious was that I was being carried. I seemed to be swinging about, and I thought I was at sea. Then there was a little jolt and a sense of pain. 'A collision,' I muttered, and opened my eyes. Beyond the fact that I seemed in a yellow world — a bright orange-yellow — my eyes did not help me, and I lay vaguely wondering about it all, till the rocking ceased. There was another bump, and then the yellow world seemed to come to an end; and as the daylight streamed in upon me I fainted again. This time when I awoke to consciousness things were clearer. I was stretched by a little stream. A native woman was sprinkling my face and washing the blood from my wounds; while another, who had with my own knife cut off my coat and shirt, was tearing the latter into strips to bandage my wounds. The yellow world was explained. I was lying on the yellow robe of one of the women. They had tied the ends together, placed a long stick through them, and carried me in the baglike hammock. They nodded to me when they saw I was conscious, and brought water in a large leaf, and poured it into my mouth. Then one went away for some time, and came back with some leaves and bark. These they chewed and put on my wounds, bound them up with strips of my shirt, and then again knotted the ends of the cloth, and lifting me up, went on as before.

"I was sure that we were much lower down the Ghaut than we had been when I was watching for the bears, and we were now going still lower. However, I knew very little Hindustani, nothing of the language the women spoke. I was too weak to stand, too weak even to think much; and I dozed and woke, and dozed again, until, after what seemed to me many hours of travel, we stopped again, this time before a tent. Two or three old women and four or five men came out, and there was great talking between them and the young women — for they were young — who had carried me down. Some of the party appeared angry; but at last things quieted down, and I was carried into the tent. I had fever, and was, I suppose, delirious for days. I afterwards found that for fully a fortnight I had lost all consciousness; but a good constitution and the nursing of the women pulled me round. When once the fever had gone, I began to mend rapidly. I tried to explain to the women that if they would go up to the camp and tell them where I was they would be well rewarded; but although I was sure they understood, they shook their heads, and by the fact that as I became stronger two or three armed men always hung about the tent, I came to the conclusion that I was a sort of prisoner. This was annoying, but did not seem serious. If these people were Dacoits, or, as was more likely, allies of the Dacoits, I could be kept only for ransom or exchange. Moreover, I felt sure of my ability to escape when I got strong, especially as I believed that in the young women who had saved my life, both by bringing me down and by their careful nursing, I should find friends."

"Were they pretty, uncle?" Mary Hastings broke in.

"Never mind whether they were pretty, Mary; they were better than pretty."

"No; but we like to know, uncle."

"Well, except for the soft, dark eyes, common to the race, and the good temper and lightheartedness, also so general among Hindu girls, and the tenderness which women feel towards a creature whose life they have saved, whether it is a wounded bird or a drowning puppy, I suppose they were nothing remarkable in the way of beauty, but at the time I know that I thought them charming.

CHAPTER II.

"Just as I was getting strong enough to walk, and was beginning to think of making my escape, a band of five or six fellows, armed to the teeth, came in, and made signs that I was to go with them. It was evidently an arranged thing, the girls only were surprised, but they were at once turned out, and as we started I could see two crouching figures in the shade with their cloths over their heads. I had a native garment thrown over my shoulders, and in five minutes after the arrival of the fellows found myself on my way. It took us some six hours before we reached our destination, which was one of those natural rock citadels. Had I been in my usual health I could have done the distance in an hour and a half, but I had to rest constantly, and was finally carried rather than helped up. I had gone not unwillingly, for the men were clearly, by their dress, Dacoits of the Deccan, and I had no doubt that it was intended either to ransom or exchange me.

"At the foot of this natural castle were some twenty or thirty more robbers, and I was led to a rough sort of arbour in which was lying, on a pile of maize straw, a man who was evidently their chief. He rose and we exchanged salaams.

"'What is your name, sahib?' he asked in Mahratta.

"'Hastings — Lieutenant Hastings,' I said. 'And yours?'

"'Sivajee Punt!' he said.

"This was bad. I had fallen into the hands of the most trouble-some, most ruthless, and most famous of the Dacoit leaders. Over and over again he had been hotly chased, but had always managed to get away; and when I last heard anything of what was going on four or five troops of native police were scouring the country after him. He gave an order which I did not understand, and a wretched Bombay writer, I suppose a clerk of some money-lender, was dragged forward. Sivajee Punt spoke to him for some time, and the fellow then told me in English that I was to write at once to the officer commanding the troops, telling him that I was in his hands, and should be put to death directly he was attacked.

"'Ask him,' I said, 'if he will take any sum of money to let me go?'

"Sivajee shook his head very decidedly.

"A piece of paper was put before me, and a pen and ink, and I wrote as I had been ordered, adding, however, in French, that I had brought myself into my present position by my own folly, and would take my chance, for I well knew the importance which Government attached to Sivajee's capture. I read out loud all that I had written in English, and the interpreter translated it. Then the paper was folded and I addressed it, 'The Officer Commanding,' and I was given some chupattis and a drink of water, and allowed to sleep. The Dacoits had apparently no fear of any immediate attack.

"It was still dark, although morning was just breaking, when I was awakened, and was got up to the citadel. I was hoisted rather than climbed, two men standing above with a rope, tied round my body, so that I was half hauled, half pushed up the difficult places, which would have taxed all my climbing powers had I been in health.

"The height of this mass of rock was about a hundred feet; the top was fairly flat, with some depressions and risings, and about eighty feet long by fifty wide. It had evidently been used as a fortress in ages past. Along the side facing the hill were the remains of a rough wall. In the centre of a depression was a cistern, some four feet square, lined with stonework, and in another depression a gallery had been cut, leading to a subterranean storeroom or chamber. This natural fortress rose from the face of the hill at a distance of a thousand yards or so from the edge of the plateau, which was fully two hundred feet higher than the top of the rock. In the old days it would have been impregnable, and even at that time it was an awkward place to take, for the troops were armed only with Brown Bess, and rifled cannon were not thought of. Looking round, I could see that I was some four miles from the point where I had descended. The camp was gone; but running my eye along the edge of the plateau I could see the tops of tents a mile to my right, and again two miles to my left; turning round, and looking down into the wide valley, I saw a regimental camp.

"It was evident that a vigorous effort was being made to surround and capture the Dacoits, since troops had been brought up from Bombay. In addition to the troops above and below, there would probably be a strong police force, acting on the face of the hill. I did not see all these things at the time, for I was, as soon as I got to the top, ordered to sit down behind the parapet, a fellow armed to the teeth squatting down by me, and signifying that if I showed my head above the stones he would cut my throat without hesitation. There were, however, sufficient gaps between the stones to allow me to have a view of the crest of the Ghaut, while below my view extended down to the hills behind Bombay. It was evident to me now why the Dacoits did not climb up into the fortress. There were dozens of similar crags on the face of the Ghauts, and the troops did not as yet know their whereabouts. It was a sort of blockade of the whole face of the hills which was being kept up, and there were, probably enough, several other bands of Dacoits lurking in the jungle.

"There were only two guards and myself on the rock plateau. I discussed with myself the chances of my overpowering them and holding the top of the rock till help came; but I was greatly weakened, and was not a match for a boy, much less for the two stalwart Mahrattas; besides, I was by no means sure that the way I had been brought up was the only possible path to the top. The day passed off quietly. The heat on the bare rock was frightful, but one of the men, seeing how weak and ill I really was, fetched a thick rug from the storehouse, and with the aid of a stick made a sort of lean-to against the wall, under which I lay sheltered from the sun.

"Once or twice during the day I heard a few distant musket-shots, and once a sharp heavy outburst of firing. It must have been three or four miles away, but it was on the side of the Ghaut, and showed that the troops or police were at work. My guards looked anxiously in that direction, and uttered sundry curses. When it was dusk, Sivajee and eight of the Dacoits came up. From what they said, I gathered that the rest of the band had dispersed, trusting either to get through the line of their pursuers, or, if caught, to escape with slight punishment, the men who remained being too deeply concerned in murderous outrages to hope for mercy. Sivajee himself handed me a letter, which the man who had taken my note had brought back in reply. Major Knapp, the writer, who was the second in command, said that he could not engage the Government, but that if Lieutenant Hastings was given up the act would certainly dispose the Government to take the most merciful view possible; but that if, on the contrary, any harm was suffered by Lieutenant Hastings, every man taken would be at once hung. Sivajee did not appear put out about it. I do not think he expected any other answer, and imagine that his real object in writing was simply to let them know that I was a prisoner, and so enable him the better to paralyse the attack upon a position which he no doubt considered all but impregnable.

"I was given food, and was then allowed to walk as I chose upon the little plateau, two of the Dacoits taking post as sentries at the steepest part of the path, while the rest gathered, chatting and smoking, in the depression in front of the storehouse. It was still light enough for me to see for some distance down the face of the rock, and I strained my eyes to see if I could discern any other spot at which an ascent or descent was possible. The prospect was not encouraging. At some places the face fell sheer away from the edge, and so evident was the impracticability of escape that the only place which I glanced at twice was the western side, that is the one away from the hill. Here it sloped gradually for a few feet. I took off my shoes and went down to the edge. Below, some ten feet, was a ledge, on to which with care I could get down, but below that was a sheer fall of some fifty feet. As a means of escape it was hopeless, but it struck me that if an attack was made I might slip away and get on to the ledge. Once there I could not be seen except by a person standing where I now was, just on the edge of the slope, a spot to which it was very unlikely that anyone would come.

"The thought gave me a shadow of hope, and, returning to the upper end of the platform, I lay down, and in spite of the hardness of the rock, was soon asleep. The pain of my aching bones woke me up several times, and once, just as the first tinge of dawn was coming, I thought I could hear movements in the jungle. I raised myself somewhat, and I saw that the sounds had been heard by the Dacoits, for they were standing listening, and some of them were bringing spare firearms from the storehouse, in evident preparation for attack.

"As I afterwards learned, the police had caught one of the Dacoits trying to effect his escape, and by means of a little of the ingenious torture to which the Indian police then frequently resorted, when their white officers were absent, they obtained from him the exact position of Sivajee's band, and learned the side from which the ascent must be made. That the Dacoit and his band were still upon the slopes of the Ghauts they knew, and were gradually narrowing their circle, but there were so many rocks and hiding places that the process of searching was a slow one, and the intelligence was so important that the news was off at once to the colonel, who gave orders for the police to surround the rock at daylight and to storm it if possible. The garrison was so small that the police were alone ample for the work, supposing that the natural difficulties were not altogether insuperable.

"Just at daybreak there was a distant noise of men moving in the jungle, and the Dacoit halfway down the path fired his gun. He was answered by a shout and a volley. The Dacoits hurried out from the chamber, and lay down on the edge, where, sheltered by a parapet, they commanded the path. They paid no attention to me, and I kept as far away as possible. The fire began — a quiet, steady fire, a shot at a time, and in strong contrast to the rattle kept up from the surrounding jungle; but every shot must have told, as man after man who strove to climb that steep path, fell. It lasted only ten minutes, and then all was quiet again.

"The attack had failed, as I knew it must do, for two men could have held the place against an army; a quarter of an hour later a gun from the crest above spoke out, and a round shot whistled above our heads. Beyond annoyance, an artillery fire could do no harm, for the party could be absolutely safe in the store cave. The instant the shot flew overhead, however, Sivajee Punt beckoned to me, and motioned me to take my seat on the wall facing the guns. Hesitation was useless, and I took my seat with my back to the Dacoits and my face to the hill. One of the Dacoits, as I did so, pulled off the native cloth which covered my shoulders, in order that I might be clearly seen.

"Just as I took my place another round shot hummed by; but then there was a long interval of silence. With a fieldglass every feature must have been distinguishable to the gunners, and I had no doubt that they were waiting for orders as to what to do next.

"I glanced round and saw that with the exception of one fellow squatted behind the parapet some half dozen yards away, clearly as a sentry to keep me in place, all the others had disappeared. Some, no doubt, were on sentry down the path, the others were in the store beneath me. After half an hour's silence the guns spoke out again. Evidently the gunners were told to be as careful as they could, for some of the shots went wide on the left, others on the right. A few struck the rock below me. The situation was not pleasant, but I thought that at a thousand yards they ought not to hit me, and I tried to distract my attention by thinking out what I should do under every possible contingency.

"Presently I felt a crash and a shock, and fell backwards to the ground. I was not hurt, and on picking myself up saw that the ball had struck the parapet to the left, just where my guard was sitting, and he lay covered with its fragments. His turban lay some yards behind him. Whether he was dead or not I neither knew nor cared.

"I pushed down some of the parapet where I had been sitting, dropped my cap on the edge outside, so as to make it appear that I had fallen over, and then picking up the man's turban, ran to the other end of the platform and scrambled down to the ledge. Then I began to wave my arms about — I had nothing on above the waist — and in a moment I saw a face with a uniform cap peer out through the jungle, and a hand was waved. I made signs to him to make his way to the foot of the perpendicular wall of rock beneath me. I then unwound the turban, whose length was, I knew, amply sufficient to reach to the bottom, and then looked round for something to write on. I had my pencil still in my trousers pocket, but not a scrap of paper.

"I picked up a flattish piece of rock and wrote on it, 'Get a rope-ladder quickly, I can haul it up. Ten men in garrison. They are all under cover. Keep on firing to distract their attention.'"

"I tied the stone to the end of the turban, and looked over. A noncommissioned officer of the police was already standing below. I lowered the stone; he took it, waved his hand to me, and was gone.

"An hour passed: it seemed an age. The round shots still rang overhead, and the fire was now much more heavy and sustained than before. Presently I again saw a movement in the jungle, and Norworthy's face appeared, and he waved his arm in greeting.

"Five minutes more and a party were gathered at the foot of the rock, and a strong rope was tied to the cloth. I pulled it up. A rope-ladder was attached to it, and the top rung was in a minute or two in my hands. To it was tied a piece of paper with the words: 'Can you fasten the ladder?" I wrote on the paper: 'No; but I can hold it for a light weight.'

"I put the paper with a stone in the end of the cloth, and lowered it again. Then I sat down, tied the rope round my waist, got my feet against two projections, and waited. There was a jerk, and then I felt some one was coming up the rope-ladder. The strain was far less than I expected, but the native policeman who came up first did not weigh half so much as an average Englishman. There were now two of us to hold. The officer in command of the police came up next, then Norworthy, then a dozen more police. I explained the situation, and we mounted to the upper level. Not a soul was to be seen. Quickly we advanced and took up a position to command the door of the underground chamber; while one of the police waved a white cloth from his bayonet as a signal to the gunners to cease firing. Then the police officer hailed the party within the cave.

"'Sivajee Punt! you may as well come out and give yourself up! We are in possession, and resistance is useless!'

"A yell of rage and surprise was heard, and the Dacoits, all desperate men, came bounding out, firing as they did so. Half of their number were shot down at once, and the rest, after a short, sharp struggle, were bound hand and foot.

"That is pretty well all of the story, I think. Sivajee Punt was one of the killed. The prisoners were all either hung or imprisoned for life. I escaped my blowing-up for having gone down the Ghauts after the bear, because, after all, Sivajee Punt might have defied their force for months had I not done so.

"It seemed that that scoundrel Rahman had taken back word that I was killed. Norworthy had sent down a strong party, who found the two dead bears, and who, having searched everywhere without finding any signs of my body, came to the conclusion that I had been found and carried away, especially as they ascertained that natives used that path. They had offered rewards, but nothing was heard of me till my note saying I was in Sivajee's hands arrived."

"And did you ever see the women who carried you off?"

"No, Mary, I never saw them again. I did, however, after immense trouble, succeed in finding out where it was that I had been taken to. I went down at once, but found the village deserted. Then after much inquiry I found where the people had moved to, and sent messages to the women to come up to the camp, but they never came; and I was reduced at last to sending them down two sets of silver bracelets, necklaces, and bangles, which must have rendered them the envy of all the women on the Ghauts. They sent back a message of grateful thanks, and I never heard of them afterwards. No doubt their relatives, who knew that their connection with the Dacoits was now known, would not let them come. However, I had done all I could, and I have no doubt the women were perfectly satisfied. So you see, my dear, that the Indian bear, small as he is, is an animal which it is as well to leave alone, at any rate when he happens to be up on the side of a hill while you are at the foot."

THE PATERNOSTERS

A YACHTING STORY

AND do you really mean that we are to cross by the steamer, Mr. Virtue, while you go over in the *Seabird?* I do not approve of that at all. Fanny, why do you not rebel, and say we won't be put ashore? I call it horrid, after a fortnight on board this dear little yacht, to have to get on to a crowded steamer, with no accommodation and lots of seasick women, perhaps, and crying children. You surely cannot be in earnest?"

"I do not like it any more than you do, Minnie; but, as Tom says we had better do it, and my husband agrees with him, I am afraid we must submit. Do you really think it is quite necessary, Mr. Virtue? Minnie and I are both good sailors, you know; and we would much rather have a little extra tossing about on board the *Seabird* than the discomforts of a steamer."

"I certainly think that it will be best, Mrs. Grantham. You know very well we would rather have you on board, and that we shall suffer from your loss more than you will by going the other way; but there's no doubt the wind is getting up, and though we don't feel it much here, it must be blowing pretty hard outside. The *Seabird* is as good a sea-boat as anything of her size that floats; but you don't know what it is to be out in anything like a heavy sea in a thirty-tonner. It would be impossible for you to stay on deck, and we should have our hands full, and should not be able to give you the benefit of our society. Personally, I should not mind being out in the *Seabird* in any weather, but I would certainly rather not have ladies on board."

"You don't think we should scream, or do anything foolish, Mr. Virtue?" Minnie Graham said indignantly.

"Not at all, Miss Graham. Still, I repeat, the knowledge that there are women on board, delightful at other times, does not tend to comfort in bad weather. Of course, if you prefer it, we can put off our start till this puff of wind has blown itself out. It may have dropped before morning. It may last some little time. I don't think myself that it will drop, for the glass has fallen, and I am afraid we may have a spell of broken weather."

"Oh no; don't put it off," Mrs. Grantham said; "we have only another fortnight before James must be back again in London, and it would be a great pity to lose three or four days perhaps; and we have been looking forward to cruising about among the Channel Islands, and to St. Malo, and all those places. Oh no; I think the other is much the better plan — that is, if you won't take us with you."

"It would be bad manners to say that I won't, Mrs. Grantham; but I must say I would rather not. It will be a very short separation. Grantham will take you on shore at once, and as soon as the boat comes back I shall be off. You will start in the steamer this evening, and get into Jersey at nine or ten o'clock tomorrow morning; and if I am not there before you, I shall not be many hours after you."

"Well, if it must be it must," Mrs. Grantham said, with an air of resignation. "Come, Minnie, let us put a few things into a handbag for tonight. You see the skipper is not to be moved by our pleadings."

"That is the worst of you married women, Fanny," Miss Graham said, with a little pout. "You get into the way of doing as you are ordered. I call it too bad. Here have we been cruising about for the last fortnight, with scarcely a breath of wind, and longing for a good brisk breeze and a little change and excitement, and now it comes at last, we are to be packed off in a steamer. I call it horrid of you, Mr. Virtue. You may laugh, but I do."

Tom Virtue laughed, but he showed no signs of giving way, and ten minutes later Mr. and Mrs. Grantham and Miss Graham took their places in the gig, and were rowed into Southampton Harbour, off which the *Seabird* was lying.

The last fortnight had been a very pleasant one, and it had cost the owner of the *Seabird* as much as his guests to come to the conclusion that it was better to break up the party for a few hours.

Tom Virtue had, up to the age of five-and-twenty, been possessed of a sufficient income for his wants. He had entered at the bar, not that he felt any particular vocation in that direction, but because he thought it incumbent upon him to do something. Then, at the death of an uncle, he had come into a considerable fortune, and was able to indulge his taste for yachting, which was the sole amusement for which he really cared, to the fullest.

He sold the little five-tonner he had formerly possessed, and purchased the *Seabird*. He could well have afforded a much larger craft, but he knew that there was far more real enjoyment in sailing to be obtained from a small craft than a large one, for in the latter he would be obliged to have a regular skipper, and would be little more than a passenger, whereas on board the *Seabird*, although his first hand was dignified by the name of skipper, he was himself the absolute master. The boat carried the aforesaid skipper, three hands, and a steward, and with them he had twice been up the Mediterranean, across to Norway, and had several times made the circuit of the British Isles.

He had unlimited confidence in his boat, and cared not what weather he was out in her. This was the first time since his ownership of her that the *Seabird* had carried lady passengers. His friend Grantham, an old school and college chum, was a hard-working barrister, and Virtue had proposed to him to take a month's holiday on board the *Seabird*.

"Put aside your books, old man," he said. "You look fagged and overworked; a month's blow will do you all the good in the world."

"Thank you, Tom; I have made up my mind for a month's holiday, but I can't accept your invitation, though I should enjoy it of all things. But it would not be fair to my wife; she doesn't get very much of my society, and she has been looking forward to our having a run together. So I must decline."

Virtue hesitated a moment. He was not very fond of ladies' society, and thought them especially in the way on board a yacht; but he had a great liking for his friend's wife, and was almost as much at home in his house as in his own chambers.

"Why not bring the wife with you?" he said, as soon as his mind was made up. "It will be a nice change for her too; and I have heard her say that she is a good sailor. The accommodation is not extensive, but the after-cabin is a pretty good size, and I would do all I could to make her comfortable. Perhaps she would like another lady with her; if so by all means bring one. They could have the after-cabin, you could have the little stateroom, and I could sleep in the saloon."

"It is very good of you, Tom, especially as I know that it will put you out frightfully; but the offer is a very tempting one. I will speak to Fanny, and let you have an answer in the morning."

"That will be delightful, James," Mrs. Grantham said, when the invitation was repeated to her. "I should like it of all things; and I am sure the rest and quiet and the sea air will be just the thing for you. It is wonderful, Tom Virtue making the offer; and I take it as a great personal compliment, for he certainly is not what is generally called a lady's man. It is very nice, too, of him to think of my having another lady on board. Whom shall we ask? Oh, I know," she said suddenly; "that will be the thing of all others. We will ask my cousin Minnie; she is full of fun and life, and will make a charming wife for Tom!"

James Grantham laughed.

"What schemers you all are, Fanny! Now I should call it downright treachery to take anyone on board the *Seabird* with the idea of capturing its master."

"Nonsense, treachery!" Mrs. Grantham said indignantly; "Minnie is the nicest girl I know, and it would do Tom a world of good to have a wife to look after him. Why, he is thirty now, and will be settling down into a confirmed old bachelor before long. It's the greatest kindness we could do him, to take Minnie on board; and I am sure he is the sort of man any girl might fall in love with when she gets to know him. The fact is, he's shy! He never had any sisters, and spends all his time in winter at that horrid club; so that really he has never had any women's society, and even with us he will never come unless he knows we are alone. I call it a great pity, for I don't know a pleasanter fellow than he is. I think it will be doing him a real service in asking Minnie; so that's settled. I will sit down and write him a note."

"In for a penny, in for a pound, I suppose," was Tom Virtue's comment when he received Mrs. Grantham's letter, thanking him warmly for the invitation, and saying that she would bring her cousin, Miss Graham, with her, if that young lady was disengaged.

As a matter of self-defence he at once invited Jack Harvey, who was a mutual friend of himself and Grantham, to be of the party.

"Jack can help Grantham to amuse the women," he said to himself; "that will be more in his line than mine. I will run down to Cowes tomorrow and have a chat with Johnson; we shall want a different sort of stores altogether to those we generally carry, and I suppose we must do her up a bit below."

Having made up his mind to the infliction of female passengers, Tom Virtue did it handsomely, and when the party came on board at Ryde they were delighted with the aspect of the yacht below. She had been repainted, the saloon and ladies' cabin were decorated in delicate shades of gray, picked out with gold; and the upholsterer, into whose hands the owner of the *Seabird* had placed her, had done his work with taste and judgment, and the ladies' cabin resembled a little boudoir.

"Why, Tom, I should have hardly known her!" Grantham, who had often spent a day on board the *Seabird*, said.

"I hardly know her myself," Tom said, rather ruefully; "but I hope she's all right, Mrs. Grantham, and that you and Miss Graham will find everything you want."

"It is charming!" Mrs. Grantham said enthusiastically. "It's awfully good of you, Tom, and we appreciate it; don't we, Minnie? It is such a surprise, too; for James said that while I should find everything very comfortable, I must not expect that a small yacht would be got up like a palace."

So a fortnight had passed; they had cruised along the coast as far as Plymouth, anchoring at night at the various ports on the way. Then they had returned to Southampton, and it had been settled that as none of the party, with the exception of Virtue himself, had been to the Channel Islands, the last fortnight of the trip should be spent there. The weather had been delightful, save that there had been some deficiency in wind, and throughout the cruise the *Seabird* had been under all the sail she could spread. But when the gentlemen came on deck early in the morning a considerable change had taken place; the sky was gray and the clouds flying fast overhead.

"We are going to have dirty weather," Tom Virtue said at once. "I don't think it's going to be a gale, but there will be more sea on than will be pleasant for ladies. I tell you what, Grantham; the best thing will be for you to go on shore with the two ladies, and cross by the boat tonight. If you don't mind going directly after breakfast I will start at once, and shall be at St. Helier's as soon as you are."

And so it had been agreed, but not, as has been seen, without opposition and protest on the part of the ladies.

Mrs. Grantham's chief reason for objecting had not been

given. The little scheme on which she had set her mind seemed to be working satisfactorily. From the first day Tom Virtue had exerted himself to play the part of host satisfactorily, and had ere long shaken off any shyness he may have felt towards the one stranger of the party, and he and Miss Graham had speedily got on friendly terms. So things were going on as well as Mrs. Grantham could have expected.

No sooner had his guests left the side of the yacht than her owner began to make his preparations for a start.

"What do you think of the weather, Watkins?" he asked his skipper.

"It's going to blow hard, sir; that's my view of it, and if I was you I shouldn't up anchor today. Still, it's just as you likes; the *Seabird* won't mind it if we don't. She has had a rough time of it before now; still, it will be a case of wet jackets, and no mistake "

"Yes, I expect we shall have a rough time of it, Watkins, but I want to get across. We don't often let ourselves be weather-bound, and I am not going to begin it today. We had better house the top-mast at once, and get two reefs in the main-sail. We can get the other down when we get clear of the island. Get number three jib up, and the leg-of-mutton mizzen; put two reefs in the foresail.'

Tom and his friend Harvey, who was a good sailor, assisted the crew in reefing down the sails, and a few minutes after the gig had returned and been hoisted in, the yawl was running rapidly down Southampton waters.

"We need hardly have reefed quite so closely," Jack Harvey said, as he puffed away at his pipe.

"Not yet, Jack; but you will see she has as much as she can carry before long. It's all the better to make all snug before starting; it saves a lot of trouble afterwards, and the extra canvas would not have made ten minutes' difference to us at the outside. We shall have pretty nearly a dead beat down the Solent. Fortunately tide will be running strong with us, but there will be a nasty kick-up there. You will see we shall feel the short choppy seas there more than we shall when we get outside. She is a grand boat in a really heavy sea, but in short waves she puts her nose into it with a will. Now, if you will take my advice, you will do as I am going to do; put on a pair of fisherman's boots and oilskin and sou'-wester. There are several sets for you to choose from below."

As her owner had predicted, the *Seabird* put her bowsprit under pretty frequently in the Solent; the wind was blowing half a gale, and as it met the tide it knocked up a short, angry sea, crested with white heads, and Jack Harvey agreed that she had quite as much sail on her as she wanted. The cabin doors were bolted, and all made snug to prevent the water getting below before they got to the race off Hurst Castle; and it was well that they did so, for she was as much under water as she was above.

"I think if I had given way to the ladies and brought them with us they would have changed their minds by this time, Jack," Tom Virtue said, with a laugh.

"I should think so," his friend agreed; "this is not a day for a fair-weather sailor. Look what a sea is breaking on the shingles!"

"Yes, five minutes there would knock her into matchwood. Another ten minutes and we shall be fairly out; and I sha'n't be sorry; one feels as if one was playing football, only just at present the *Seabird* is the ball and the waves the kickers."

Another quarter of an hour and they had passed the Needles.

"That is more pleasant, Jack," as the short, chopping motion was exchanged for a regular rise and fall; "this is what I enjoy — a steady wind and a regular sea. The *Seabird* goes over it like one of her namesakes; she is not taking a teacupful now over her bows.

"Watkins, you may as well take the helm for a spell, while we go down to lunch. I am not sorry to give it up for a bit, for it has been jerking like the kick of a horse.

"That's right, Jack, hang up your oilskin there. Johnson, give us a couple of towels; we have been pretty well smothered up there on deck. Now what have you got for us?"

"There is some soup ready, sir, and that cold pie you had for dinner yesterday."

"That will do; open a couple of bottles of stout."

Lunch, over, they went on deck again.

"She likes a good blow as well as we do," Virtue said, enthusiastically, as the yawl rose lightly over each wave. "What do you think of it, Watkins? Is the wind going to lull a bit as the sun goes down?"

"I think not, sir. It seems to me it's blowing harder than it was."

"Then we will prepare for the worst, Watkins; get the try-sail up on deck. When you are ready we will bring her up into the wind and set it. That's the comfort of a yawl, Jack; one can always lie to without any bother, and one hasn't got such a tremendous boom to handle."

The try-sail was soon on deck, and then the *Seabird* was brought up into the wind, the weather fore-sheet hauled aft, the mizzen sheeted almost fore and aft, and the *Seabird* lay, head to wind, rising and falling with a gentle motion, in strong contrast to her impetuous rushes when under sail.

"She would ride out anything like that," her owner said. "Last time we came through the Bay on our way from Gib., we were caught in a gale strong enough to blow the hair off one's head, and we lay to for nearly three days, and didn't ship a bucket of water all the time. Now let us lend a hand to get the main-sail stowed."

Ten minutes' work and it was securely fastened and its cover on; two reefs were put in the try-sail. Two hands went to each of the halliards, while, as the sail rose, Tom Virtue fastened the toggles round the mast.

"All ready, Watkins?"

"All ready, sir."

"Slack off the weather fore-sheet, then, and haul aft the leeward. Slack out the mizzen-sheet a little, Jack. That's it; now she's off again, like a duck."

The *Seabird* felt the relief from the pressure of the heavy boom to leeward and rose easily and lightly over the waves.

"She certainly is a splendid sea-boat, Tom; I don't wonder you are ready to go anywhere in her. I thought we were rather fools for starting this morning, although I enjoy a good blow; but now I don't care how hard it comes on."

By night it was blowing a downright gale.

"We will lie to till morning, Watkins. So that we get in by daylight tomorrow evening, that is all we want. See our side-lights are burning well, and you had better get up a couple of blue lights, in case anything comes running up Channel and don't see our lights. We had better divide into two watches; I will keep one with Matthews and Dawson, Mr. Harvey will go in your watch with Nicholls. We had better get the try-sail down altogether, and lie to under the foresail and mizzen, but don't put many lashings on the try-sail, one will be enough, and have it ready to cast off in a moment, in case we want to hoist the sail in a hurry. I will go down and have a glass of hot grog first, and then I will take my watch to begin with. Let the two hands with me go down; the steward will serve them out a tot each. Jack, you had better turn in at once."

Virtue was soon on deck again, muffled up in his oilskins.

"Now, Watkins, you can go below and turn in."

"I sha'n't go below tonight, sir — not to lie down. There's nothing much to do here, but I couldn't sleep, if I did lie down."

"Very well; you had better go below and get a glass of grog; tell the steward to give you a big pipe with a cover like this, out of the locker; and there's plenty of chewing tobacco, if the men are short."

"I will take that instead of a pipe," Watkins said; "there's nothing like a quid in weather like this, it ain't never in your way, and it lasts. Even with a cover a pipe would soon be out."

"Please yourself, Watkins; tell the two hands forward to keep a bright lookout for lights."

The night passed slowly. Occasionally a sea heavier than usual came on board, curling over the bow and falling with a heavy thud on the deck, but for the most part the *Seabird* breasted the waves easily; the bowsprit had been reefed in to its fullest, thereby adding to the lightness and buoyancy of the boat. Tom Virtue did not go below when his friend came up to relieve him at the change of watch, but sat smoking and doing much talking in the short intervals between the gusts.

The morning broke gray and misty, driving sleet came along on the wind, and the horizon was closed in as by a dull curtain.

"How far can we see, do you think, Watkins?"

"Perhaps a couple of miles, sir."

"That will be enough. I think we both know the position of every reef to within a hundred yards, so we will shape our course for Guernsey. If we happen to hit it off, we can hold on to St. Helier; but if when we think we ought to be within sight of Guernsey we see nothing of it, we must lie to again, till the storm has blown itself out or the clouds lift. It would never do to go groping our way along with such currents as run among the islands. Put the last reef in the try-sail before you hoist it. I think you had better get the foresail down altogether, and run up the spit-fire jib."

The *Seabird* was soon under way again.

"Now, Watkins, you take the helm; we will go down and have a cup of hot coffee, and I will see that the steward has a good supply for you and the hands; but first, do you take the helm, Jack, whilst Watkins and I have a look at the chart, and try and work out where we are, and the course we had better lie for Guernsey."

Five minutes were spent over the chart, then Watkins went up and Jack Harvey came down.

"You have got the coffee ready, I hope, Johnson?"

"Yes, sir, coffee and chocolate. I didn't know which you would like."

"Chocolate, by all means. Jack, I recommend the chocolate. Bring two full-sized bowls, Johnson, and put that cold pie on the table, and a couple of knives and forks; never mind about a cloth; but first of all bring a couple of basins of hot water, we shall enjoy our food more after a wash."

The early breakfast was eaten, dry coats and mufflers put on, pipes lighted, and they then went up upon deck. Tom took the helm.

"What time do you calculate we ought to make Guernsey, Tom?"

"About twelve. The wind is freer than it was, and we are walking along at a good pace. Matthews, cast the log, and let's see what we are doing. About seven knots, I should say."

"Seven and a quarter, sir," the man said, when he checked the line.

"Not a bad guess, Tom; it's always difficult to judge pace in a heavy sea."

At eleven o'clock the mist ceased.

"That's fortunate," Tom Virtue said; "I shouldn't be surprised if we get a glimpse of the sun between the clouds, presently. Will you get my sextant and the chronometer up, Jack, and put them handy?"

Jack Harvey did as he was asked, but there was no occasion to use the instruments, for ten minutes later, Watkins, who was standing near the bow gazing fixedly ahead, shouted:

"There's Guernsey, sir, on her lee bow, about six miles away, I should say."

"That's it, sure enough," Tom agreed, as he gazed in the direction in which Watkins was pointing. "There's a gleam of sunshine on it, or we shouldn't have seen it yet. Yes, I think you are about right as to the distance. Now let us take its bearings, we may lose it again directly."

Having taken the bearings of the island they went below, and marked off their position on the chart, and they shaped their course for Cape Grosnez, the north-western point of Jersey. The gleam of sunshine was transient — the clouds closed in again overhead, darker and grayer than before. Soon the drops of rain came flying before the wind, the horizon closed in, and they could not see half a mile away, but, though the sea was heavy, the *Seabird* was making capital weather of it, and the two friends agreed that, after all, the excitement of a sail like this was worth a month of pottering about in calms.

"We must keep a bright lookout presently," the skipper said; "there are some nasty rocks off the coast of Jersey. We must give them a wide berth. We had best make round to the south of the island, and lay to there till we can pick up a pilot to take us into St. Helier. I don't think it will be worth while trying to get into St. Aubyn's Bay by ourselves."

"I think so, too, Watkins, but we will see what it is like before it gets dark; if we can pick up a pilot all the better; if not, we will lie to till morning, if the weather keeps thick; but if it clears so that we can make out all the lights we ought to be able to get into the bay anyhow."

An hour later the rain ceased and the sky appeared somewhat clearer. Suddenly Watkins exclaimed, "There is a wreck, sir! There, three miles away to leeward. She is on the Paternosters."

"Good heavens! she is a steamer," Tom exclaimed, as he caught sight of her the next time the *Seabird* lifted on a wave. "Can she be the Southampton boat, do you think?"

"Like enough, sir, she may have had it thicker than we had, and may not have calculated enough for the current."

"Up helm, Jack, and bear away towards her. Shall we shake out a reef, Watkins?"

"I wouldn't, sir; she has got as much as she can carry on her now. We must mind what we are doing, sir; the currents run like a millstream, and if we get that reef under our lee, and the wind and current both setting us on to it, it will be all up with us in no time."

"Yes, I know that, Watkins. Jack, take the helm a minute while we run down and look at the chart.

"Our only chance, Watkins, is to work up behind the reef, and try and get so that they can either fasten a line to a buoy and let it float down to us, or get into a boat, if they have one left, and drift to us."

"They are an awful group of rocks," Watkins said, as they examined the chart; "you see some of them show merely at high tide, and a lot of them are above at low water. It will be an awful business to get among them rocks, sir, just about as near certain death as a thing can be."

"Well, it's got to be done, Watkins," Tom said, firmly. "I see the danger as well as you do, but whatever the risk, it must be tried. Mr. Grantham and the two ladies went on board by my persuasion, and I should never forgive myself if anything happened to them. But I will speak to the men."

He went on deck again and called the men to him. "Look here, lads; you see that steamer ashore on the Paternosters. In such a sea as this she may go to pieces in half an hour. I am determined to make an effort to save the lives of those on board. As you can see for yourselves there is no lying to weather of her, with the current and wind driving us on to the reef; we must beat up from behind. Now, lads, the sea there is full of rocks, and the chances are ten to one we strike on to them and go to pieces; but, anyhow I am going to try; but I won't take you unless you are willing. The boat is a good one, and the zinc chambers will keep her afloat if she fills; well managed, you ought to be able to make the coast of Jersey in her. Mr. Harvey, Watkins, and I can handle the yacht, so you can take the boat if you like."

The men replied that they would stick to the yacht wherever Mr. Virtue chose to take her, and muttered something about the ladies, for the pleasant faces of Mrs. Grantham and Miss Graham had, during the fortnight they had been on board, won the men's hearts.

"Very well, lads, I am glad to find you will stick by me; if we pull safely through it I will give each of you three months' wages. Now set to work with a will and get the gig out. We will tow her after us, and take to her if we make a smash of it."

They were now near enough to see the white breakers, in the

middle of which the ship was lying. She was fast breaking up. The jagged outline showed that the stern had been beaten in. The masts and funnel were gone, and the waves seemed to make a clean breach over her, almost hiding her from sight in a white cloud of spray.

"Wood and iron can't stand that much longer," Jack Harvey said; "another hour and I should say there won't be two planks left together."

"It is awful, Jack; I would give all I have in the world if I had not persuaded them to go on board. Keep her off a little more, Watkins."

The *Seabird* passed within a cable's-length of the breakers at the northern end of the reef.

"Now, lads, take your places at the sheets, ready to haul or let go as I give the word." So saying, Tom Virtue took his place in the bow, holding on by the forestay.

The wind was full on the *Seabird's* beam as she entered the broken water. Here and there the dark heads of the rocks showed above the water. These were easy enough to avoid, the danger lay in those hidden beneath its surface, and whose position was indicated only by the occasional break of a sea as it passed over them. Every time the *Seabird* sank on a wave those on board involuntarily held their breath, but the water here was comparatively smooth, the sea having spent its first force upon the outer reef. With a wave of his hand Tom directed the helmsman as to his course, and the little yacht was admirably handled through the dangers.

"I begin to think we shall do it," Tom said to Jack Harvey, who was standing close to him. "Another five minutes and we shall be within reach of her."

It could be seen now that there was a group of people clustered in the bow of the wreck. Two or three light lines were coiled in readiness for throwing.

"Now, Watkins," Tom said, going aft, "make straight for the wreck. I see no broken water between us and them, and possibly there may be deep water under their bow."

It was an anxious moment, as, with the sails flattened in, the yawl forged up nearly in the eye of the wind towards the wreck. Her progress was slow, for she was now stemming the current.

Tom stood with a coil of line in his hand in the bow.

"You get ready to throw, Jack, if I miss."

Nearer and nearer the yacht approached the wreck, until the bowsprit of the latter seemed to stand almost over her. Then Tom threw the line. It fell over the bowsprit, and a cheer broke from those on board the wreck and from the sailors of the *Seabird*. A stronger line was at once fastened to that thrown, and to this a strong hawser was attached.

"Down with the helm, Watkins. Now, lads, lower away the try-sail as fast as you can. Now, one of you, clear that hawser as they haul on it. Now out with the anchors."

These had been got into readiness; it was not thought that they would get any hold on the rocky bottom, still they might catch on a projecting ledge, and at any rate their weight and that of the chain cable would relieve the strain upon the hawser.

Two sailors had run out on the bowsprit of the wreck as soon as the line was thrown, and the end of the hawser was now on board the steamer.

"Thank God, there's Grantham!" Jack Harvey exclaimed; "do you see him waving his hand?"

"I see him," Tom said, "but I don't see the ladies."

"They are there, no doubt," Jack said, confidently; "crouching down, I expect. He would not be there if they weren't, you may be sure. Yes, there they are; those two muffled-up figures. There, one of them has thrown back her cloak and is waving her arm."

The two young men waved their caps.

"Are the anchors holding, Watkins? There's a tremendous strain on that hawser."

"I think so, sir; they are both tight."

"Put them round the windlass, and give a turn or two, we must relieve the strain on that hawser."

Since they had first seen the wreck the waves had made great progress in the work of destruction, and the steamer had broken in two just aft of the engines.

"Get over the spare spars, Watkins, and fasten them to float in front of her bows like a triangle. Matthews, catch hold of that boat-hook and try to fend off any piece of timber that comes along. You get hold of the sweeps, lads, and do the same. They would stave her in like a nut-shell if they struck her.

"Thank God, here comes the first of them!"

Those on board the steamer had not been idle. As soon as the yawl was seen approaching slings were prepared, and no sooner was the hawser securely fixed, than the slings were attached to it and a woman placed in them. The hawser was tight and the descent sharp, and without a check the figure ran down to the deck of the *Seabird*. She was lifted out of the slings by Tom and Jack Harvey, who found she was an old woman and had entirely lost consciousness.

"Two of you carry her down below; tell Johnson to pour a little brandy down her throat. Give her some hot soup as soon as she comes to."

Another woman was lowered and helped below. The next to descend was Mrs. Grantham.

"Thank God, you are rescued!" Tom said, as he helped her out of the sling.

"Thank God, indeed," Mrs. Grantham said, "and thank you all! Oh, Tom, we have had a terrible time of it, and had lost all hope till we saw your sail, and even then the captain said that he was afraid nothing could be done. Minnie was the first to make out it was you, and then we began to hope. She has been so brave, dear girl. Ah! here she comes."

But Minnie's firmness came to an end now that she felt the need for it was over. She was unable to stand when she was lifted from the slings; and Tom carried her below.

"Are there any more women, Mrs. Grantham?"

"No; there was only one other lady passenger and the stewardess."

"Then you had better take possession of your own cabin. I ordered Johnson to spread a couple more mattresses and some bedding on the floor, so you will all four be able to turn in. There's plenty of hot coffee and soup. I should advise soup with two or three spoonfuls of brandy in it. Now, excuse me; I must go upon deck."

Twelve men descended by the hawser, one of them with both legs broken by the fall of the mizzen. The last to come was the captain.

"Is that all?" Tom asked.

"That is all," the captain said. "Six men were swept overboard when she first struck, and two were killed by the fall of the funnel. Fortunately we had only three gentlemen passengers and three ladies on board. The weather looked so wild when we started that no one else cared about making the passage. God bless you, sir, for what you have done! Another half hour and it would have been all over with us. But it seems like a miracle your getting safe through the rocks to us."

"It was fortunate indeed that we came along," Tom said; "three of the passengers are dear friends of mine; and as it was by my persuasion that they came across in the steamer instead of in the yacht, I should never have forgiven myself if they had been lost. Take all your men below, captain; you will find plenty of hot soup there. Now, Watkins, let us be off; that steamer won't hold together many minutes longer, so there's no time to lose. We will go back as we came. Give me a hatchet. Now, lads, two of you stand at the chain-cables; knock out the shackles the moment I cut the hawser. Watkins, you take the helm and let her head pay off till the jib fills. Jack, you lend a hand to the other two, and get up the try-sail again as soon as we are free."

In a moment all were at their stations. The helm was put on the yacht, and she payed off on the opposite tack to that on which she had before been sailing. As soon as the jib filled, Tom gave two vigorous blows with his hatchet on the hawser, and, as he lifted his hand for a third, it parted. Then came the sharp rattle of the chains as they ran round the hawser-holes. The try-sail was hoisted and sheeted home, and the *Seabird* was under way again. Tom, as before, conned the ship from the bow. Several times she was in close proximity to the rocks, but each time she avoided them. A shout of gladness rose from all on deck as she passed the last patch of white water. Then she tacked and bore away for Jersey.

Tom had now time to go down below and look after his passengers. They consisted of the captain and two sailors — the sole survivors of those who had been on deck when the vessel struck — three male passengers, and six engineers and stokers.

"I have not had time to shake you by the hand before, Tom," Grantham said, as Tom Virtue entered; "and I thought you would not want me on deck at present. God bless you, old fellow! we all owe you our lives."

"How did it happen, captain?" Tom asked, as the captain also came up to him.

"It was the currents, I suppose," the captain said; "it was so thick we could not see a quarter of a mile any way. The weather was so wild I would not put into Guernsey, and passed the island without seeing it. I steered my usual course, but the gale must have altered the currents, for I thought I was three miles away from the reef, when we saw it on our beam, not a hundred yards away. It was too late to avoid it then, and in another minute we ran upon it, and the waves were sweeping over us. Every one behaved well. I got all, except those who had been swept overboard or crushed by the funnel, up into the bow of the ship, and there we waited. There was nothing to be done. No boat would live for a moment in the sea on that reef, and all I could advise was, that when she went to pieces every one should try to get hold of a floating fragment; but I doubt whether a man would have been alive a quarter of an hour after she went to pieces."

"Perhaps, captain, you will come on deck with me and give me the benefit of your advice. My skipper and I know the islands pretty well, but no doubt you know them a good deal better, and I don't want another mishap."

But the *Seabird* avoided all further dangers, and as it became dark, the lights of St. Helier's were in sight, and an hour later the yacht brought up in the port and landed her involuntary passengers.

A fortnight afterwards the *Seabird* returned to England, and two months later Mrs. Grantham had the satisfaction of being present at the ceremony which was the successful consummation of her little scheme in inviting Minnie Graham to be her companion on board the *Seabird*.

"Well, my dear," her husband said, when she indulged in a little natural triumph, "I do not say that it has not turned out well, and I am heartily glad for both Tom and Minnie's sake it has so; but you must allow that it very nearly had a disastrous ending, and I think if I were you I should leave matters to take their natural course in future. I have accepted Tom's invitation for the same party to take a cruise in the *Seabird* next summer, but I have bargained that next time a storm is brewing up we shall stop quietly in port."

"That's all very well, James," Mrs. Grantham said saucily; "but you must remember that Tom Virtue will only be first-mate of the *Seabird* in future."

"That I shall be able to tell you better, my dear, after our next cruise. All husbands are not as docile and easily led as I am."

A PIPE OF MYSTERY

A jovial party were gathered round a blazing fire in an old grange near Warwick. The hour was getting late; the very little ones had, after dancing round the Christmas tree, enjoying the snapdragon, and playing a variety of games, gone off to bed; and the elder boys and girls now gathered round their uncle, Colonel Harley, and asked him for a story — above all, a ghost story.

"But I have never seen any ghosts," the colonel said, laughing; "and, moreover, I don't believe in them one bit. I have travelled pretty well all over the world, I have slept in houses said to be haunted, but nothing have I seen — no noises that could not be accounted for by rats or the wind have I ever heard. I have never" — and here he paused — "never but once met with any circumstances or occurrence that could not be accounted for by the light of reason, and I know you prefer hearing stories of my own adventures to mere invention."

"Yes, uncle. But what was the 'once' when circumstances happened that you could not explain?"

"It's rather a long story," the colonel said, "and it's getting late."

"Oh! no, no, uncle; it does not matter a bit how late we sit up on Christmas Eve, and the longer the story is, the better; and if you don't believe in ghosts, how can it be a story of something you could not account for by the light of nature?"

"You will see when I have done," the colonel said. "It is rather a story of what the Scotch call second sight, than one of ghosts. As to accounting for it, you shall form your own opinion when you have heard me to the end.

"I landed in India in '50, and after going through the regular drill work, marched with a detachment up country to join my regiment, which was stationed at Jubbalpore, in the very heart of India. It has become an important place since; the railroad across India passes through it, and no end of changes have taken place; but at that time it was one of the most out-of-the-way stations in India, and, I may say, one of the most pleasant. It lay high, there was capital boating on the Nerbudda, and, above all, it was a grand place for sport, for it lay at the foot of the hill country, an immense district, then but little known, covered with forests and jungle, and abounding with big game of all kinds.

"My great friend there was a man named Simmonds. He was just of my own standing; we had come out in the same ship, had marched up the country together, and were almost like brothers. He was an old Etonian, I an old Westminster, and we were both fond of boating, and, indeed, of sport of all kinds. But I am not going to tell you of that now. The people in these hills are called Gonds, a true hill tribe — that is to say, aborigines, somewhat of the negro type. The chiefs are of mixed blood, but the people are almost black. They are supposed to accept the religion of the Hindus, but are in reality deplorably ignorant and superstitious. Their priests are a sort of compound of a Brahmin priest and a negro fetish man, and among their principal duties is that of charming away tigers from the villages by means of incantations. There, as in other parts of India, were a few wandering fakirs, who enjoyed an immense reputation for holiness and wisdom. The people would go to them from great distances for charms or predictions, and believed in their power with implicit faith.

"At the time when we were at Jubbalpore, there was one of these fellows, whose reputation altogether eclipsed that of his rivals, and nothing could be done until his permission had been asked and his blessing obtained. All sorts of marvellous stories were constantly coming to our ears of the unerring foresight with which he predicted the termination of diseases, both in men and animals; and so generally was he believed in that the colonel ordered that no one connected with the regiment should consult him, for these predictions very frequently brought about their own fulfilment; for those who were told that an illness would terminate fatally, lost all hope, and literally lay down to die.

"However, many of the stories that we heard could not be explained on these grounds, and the fakir and his doings were often talked over at mess, some of the officers scoffing at the whole business, others maintaining that some of these fakirs had, in some way or another, the power of foretelling the future, citing many well authenticated anecdotes upon the subject.

"The older officers were the believers, we young fellows were the scoffers. But for the well-known fact that it is very seldom indeed that these fakirs will utter any of their predictions to Europeans, some of us would have gone to him, to test his powers. As it was, none of us had ever seen him.

"He lived in an old ruined temple, in the middle of a large patch of jungle at the foot of the hills, some ten or twelve miles away.

"I had been at Jubbalpore about a year, when I was woke up one night by a native, who came in to say that at about eight o'clock a tiger had killed a man in his village, and had dragged off the body.

"Simmonds and I were constantly out after tigers, and the people in all the villages within twenty miles knew that we were always ready to pay for early information. This tiger had been doing great damage, and had carried off about thirty men, women, and children. So great was the fear of him, indeed, that the people in the neighbourhood he frequented scarcely dared stir out of doors, except in parties of five or six. We had had several hunts after him, but, like all man-eaters, he was old and awfully crafty; and although we got several snap shots at him, he had always managed to save his skin.

"In a quarter of an hour after the receipt of the message, Charley Simmonds and I were on the back of an elephant, which was our joint property; our shekarry, a capital fellow, was on foot beside us, and with the native trotting on ahead as guide we went off at the best pace of old Begaum, for that was the elephant's name. The village was fifteen miles away, but we got there soon after daybreak, and were received with delight by the population. In half an hour the hunt was organized; all the male population turned out as beaters, with sticks, guns, tomtoms, and other instruments for making a noise.

"The trail was not difficult to find. A broad path, with occasional smears of blood, showed where he had dragged his victim through the long grass to a cluster of trees a couple of hundred yards from the village.

"We scarcely expected to find him there, but the villagers held back, while we went forward with cocked rifles. We found, however, nothing but a few bones and a quantity of blood. The tiger had made off at the approach of daylight into the jungle, which was about two miles distant. We traced him easily enough, and found that he had entered a large ravine, from which several smaller ones branched off.

"It was an awkward place, as it was next to impossible to surround it with the number of people at our command. We posted them at last all along the upper ground, and told them to make up in noise what they wanted in numbers. At last all was ready, and we gave the signal. However, I am not telling you a hunting story, and need only say that we could neither find nor disturb him. In vain we pushed Begaum through the thickest of the jungle which clothed the sides and bottom of the ravine, while the men shouted, beat their tomtoms, and showered imprecations against the tiger himself and his ancestors up to the remotest generations.

"The day was tremendously hot, and, after three hours' march, we gave it up for a time, and lay down in the shade, while the shekarries made a long examination of the ground all round the hillside, to be sure that he had not left the ravine. They came back with the news that no traces could be discovered, and that, beyond a doubt, he was still there. A tiger will crouch up in an exceedingly small clump of grass or bush, and will sometimes almost allow himself to be trodden on before moving. However, we determined to have one more search, and if that should prove unsuccessful, to send off to Jubbalpore for some more of the men to come out with elephants, while we kept up a circle of fires, and of noises of all descriptions, so as to keep him a prisoner until the arrival of the reinforcements. Our next search was no more successful than our first had been; and having, as we imagined, examined every clump and crevice in which he could have been concealed, we had just reached the upper end of the ravine, when we heard a tremendous roar, followed by a perfect babel of yells and screams from the natives.

"The outburst came from the mouth of the ravine, and we felt at once that he had escaped. We hurried back to find, as we had expected, that the tiger was gone. He had burst out suddenly from his hiding place, had seized a native, torn him horribly, and had made across the open plain.

"This was terribly provoking, but we had nothing to do but follow him. This was easy enough, and we traced him to a detached patch of wood and jungle, two miles distant. This wood was four or five hundred yards across, and the exclamations of the people at once told us that it was the one in which stood the ruined temple of the fakir of whom I have been telling you. I forgot to say, that as the tiger broke out one of the village shekarries had fired at, and, he declared, wounded him.

"It was already getting late in the afternoon, and it was hopeless to attempt to beat the jungle that night. We therefore sent off a runner with a note to the colonel, asking him to send the work-elephants, and to allow a party of volunteers to march over at night, to help surround the jungle when we commenced beating it in the morning.

"We based our request upon the fact that the tiger was a notorious man-eater, and had been doing immense damage. We then had a talk with our shekarry, sent a man off to bring provisions for the people out with us, and then set them to work cutting sticks and grass to make a circle of fires.

"We both felt much uneasiness respecting the fakir, who might be seized at any moment by the enraged tiger. The natives would not allow that there was any cause for fear, as the tiger would not dare to touch so holy a man. Our belief in the respect of the tiger for sanctity was by no means strong, and we determined to go in and warn him of the presence of the brute in the wood. It was a mission which we could not intrust to anyone else, for no native would have entered the jungle for untold gold; so we mounted the Begaum again, and started. The path leading towards the temple was pretty wide, and as we went along almost noiselessly, for the elephant was too well trained to tread upon fallen sticks, it was just possible we might come upon the tiger suddenly, so we kept our rifles in readiness in our hands.

"Presently we came in sight of the ruins. No one was at first visible; but at that very moment the fakir came out from the temple. He did not see or hear us, for we were rather behind him and still among the trees, but at once proceeded in a high voice to break into a singsong prayer. He had not said two words before his voice was drowned in a terrific roar, and in an instant the tiger had sprung upon him, struck him to the ground, seized him as a cat would a mouse, and started off with him at a trot. The brute evidently had not detected our presence, for he came right towards us. We halted the Begaum, and with our fingers on the triggers, awaited the favourable moment. He was a hundred yards from us when he struck down his victim; he was not more than fifty when he caught sight of us. He stopped for an instant in surprise. Charley muttered, 'Both barrels, Harley,' and as the beast turned to plunge into the jungle, and so showed us his side, we sent four bullets crashing into him, and he rolled over lifeless.

"We went up to the spot, made the Begaum give him a kick, to be sure that he was dead, and then got down to examine the unfortunate fakir. The tiger had seized him by the shoulder, which was terribly torn, and the bone broken. He was still perfectly conscious.

"We at once fired three shots, our usual signal that the tiger was dead, and in a few minutes were surrounded by the villagers, who hardly knew whether to be delighted at the death of their enemy, or to grieve over the injury to the fakir. We proposed taking the latter to our hospital at Jubbalpore, but this he positively refused to listen to. However we finally persuaded him to allow his arm to be set and the wounds dressed in the first place by our regimental surgeon, after which he could go to one of the native villages and have his arm dressed in accordance with his own notions. A litter was soon improvised, and away we went to Jubbalpore, which we reached about eight in the evening.

"The fakir refused to enter the hospital, so we brought out a couple of trestles, laid the litter upon them, and the surgeon set his arm and dressed his wounds by torchlight, when he was lifted into a dhoolie, and his bearers again prepared to start for the village.

"Hitherto he had only spoken a few words; but he now briefly expressed his deep gratitude to Simmonds and myself. We told him that we would ride over to see him shortly, and hoped to find him getting on rapidly. Another minute and he was gone.

"It happened that we had three or four fellows away on leave or on staff duty, and several others knocked up with fever just about this time, so that the duty fell very heavily upon the rest of us, and it was over a month before we had time to ride over to see the fakir.

"We had heard he was going on well; but we were surprised, on reaching the village, to find that he had already returned to his old abode in the jungle. However, we had made up our minds to see him, especially as we had agreed that we would endeavour to persuade him to do a prediction for us; so we turned our horses' heads towards the jungle. We found the fakir sitting on a rock in front of the temple, just where he had been seized by the tiger. He rose as we rode up.

"'I knew that you would come today, sahibs, and was joyful in the thought of seeing those who have preserved my life.'

"'We are glad to see you looking pretty strong again, though your arm is still in a sling,' I said, for Simmonds was not strong in Hindustani.

"'How did you know that we were coming?' I asked, when we had tied up our horses.

"'Siva has given to his servant to know many things,' he said quietly.

"'Did you know beforehand that the tiger was going to seize you?' I asked.

"'I knew that a great danger threatened, and that Siva would not let me die before my time had come.'

"'Could you see into our future?' I asked.

"The fakir hesitated, looked at me for a moment earnestly to see if I was speaking in mockery, and then said:

"'The sahibs do not believe in the power of Siva or of his servants. They call his messengers impostors, and scoff at them when they speak of the events of the future.'

"'No, indeed,' I said. 'My friend and I have no idea of scoffing. We have heard of so many of your predictions coming true, that we are really anxious that you should tell us something of the future.'

"The fakir nodded his head, went into the temple, and returned in a minute or two with two small pipes used by the natives for opium smoking, and a brazier of burning charcoal. The pipes were already charged. He made signs to us to sit down, and took his place in front of us. Then he began singing in a low voice, rocking himself to and fro, and waving a staff which he held in his hand. Gradually his voice rose, and his gesticulations and actions became more violent. So far as I could make out, it was a prayer to Siva that he would give some glimpse of the future which might benefit the sahibs who had saved the life of his servant. Presently he darted forward, gave us each a pipe, took two pieces of red-hot charcoal from the brazier in his fingers, without seeming to know that they were warm, and placed them in the pipes; then he recommenced his singing and gesticulations.

"A glance at Charley, to see if, like myself, he was ready to carry the thing through, and then I put the pipe to my lips. I felt at once that it was opium, of which I had before made experiment, but mixed with some other substance, which was, I imagine, haschish, a preparation of hemp. A few puffs, and I felt a drowsiness creeping over me. I saw, as through a mist, the fakir swaying himself backwards and forwards, his arms waving, and his face distorted. Another minute, and the pipe slipped from my fingers, and I fell back insensible.

"How long I lay there I do not know. I woke with a strange and not unpleasant sensation, and presently became conscious that the fakir was gently pressing, with a sort of shampooing action, my temples and head. When he saw that I opened my eyes he left me, and performed the same process upon Charley. In a few minutes he rose from his stooping position, waved his hand in token of adieu, and walked slowly back into the temple.

"As he disappeared I sat up; Charley did the same.

"We stared at each other for a minute without speaking, and then Charley said:

"'This is a rum go, and no mistake, old man.'

"'You're right, Charley. My opinion is, we've made fools of ourselves. Let's be off out of this.'

"We staggered to our feet, for we both felt like drunken men, made our way to our horses, poured a mussuk of water over our heads, took a drink of brandy from our flasks, and then feeling more like ourselves, mounted and rode out of the jungle.

"'Well, Harley, if the glimpse of futurity which I had is true, all I can say is that it was extremely unpleasant.'

"'That was just my case, Charley.'

"'My dream, or whatever you like to call it, was about a mutiny of the men.'

"'You don't say so, Charley; so was mine. This is monstrously strange, to say the least of it. However, you tell your story first, and then I will tell mine.'

"'It was very short,' Charley said. 'We were at mess — not in our present mess-room — we were dining with the fellows of some other regiment. Suddenly, without any warning, the windows were filled with a crowd of Sepoys, who opened fire right and left into us. Half the fellows were shot down at once; the rest of us made a rush to our swords just as the niggers came swarming into the room. There was a desperate fight for a moment. I remember that Subadar Pirán — one of the best native officers in the regiment, by the way — made a rush at me, and I shot him through the head with a revolver. At the same moment a ball hit me, and down I went. At the moment a Sepoy fell dead across me, hiding me partly from sight. The fight lasted a minute or two longer. I fancy a few fellows escaped, for I heard shots outside. Then the place became quiet. In another minute I heard a crackling, and saw that the devils had set the mess-room on fire. One of our men, who was lying close by me, got up and crawled to the window, but he was shot down the moment he showed himself. I was hesitating whether to do the same or to lie still and be smothered, when suddenly I rolled the dead sepoy off, crawled into the anteroom half suffocated by smoke, raised the lid of a very heavy trapdoor, and stumbled down some steps into a place, half storehouse half cellar, under the mess-room. How I knew about it being there I don't know. The trap closed over my head with a bang. That is all I remember.'

"'Well, Charley, curiously enough my dream was also about an extraordinary escape from danger, lasting, like yours, only a minute or two. The first thing I remember — there seems to have been something before, but what, I don't know — I was on horseback, holding a very pretty but awfully pale girl in front of me. We were pursued by a whole troop of Sepoy cavalry, who were firing pistol shots at us. We were not more than seventy or eighty yards in front, and they were gaining fast, just as I rode into a large deserted temple. In the centre was a huge stone figure. I jumped off my horse with the lady, and as I did so she said, 'Blow out my brains, Edward; don't let me fall alive into their hands.'

"'Instead of answering, I hurried her round behind the idol, pushed against one of the leaves of a flower in the carving, and the stone swung back, and showed a hole just large enough to get through, with a stone staircase inside the body of the idol, made no doubt for the priest to go up and give responses through the mouth. I hurried the girl through, crept in after her, and closed the stone, just as our pursuers came clattering into the courtyard. That is all I remember.'

"'Well, it is monstrously rum,' Charley said, after a pause.

'Did you understand what the old fellow was singing about before he gave us the pipes?'

"'Yes; I caught the general drift. It was an entreaty to Siva to give us some glimpse of futurity which might benefit us.'

"We lit our cheroots and rode for some miles at a brisk canter without remark. When we were within a short distance of home we reined up.

"'I feel ever so much better,' Charley said. 'We have got that opium out of our heads now. How do you account for it all, Harley?'

"'I account for it in this way, Charley. The opium naturally had the effect of making us both dream, and as we took similar doses of the same mixture, under similar circumstances, it is scarcely extraordinary that it should have effected the same portion of the brain, and caused a certain similarity in our dreams. In all nightmares something terrible happens, or is on the point of happening; and so it was here. Not unnaturally in both our cases, our thoughts turned to soldiers. If you remember there was a talk at mess some little time since, as to what would happen in the extremely unlikely event of the sepoys mutinying in a body. I have no doubt that was the foundation of both our dreams. It is all natural enough when we come to think it over calmly. I think, by the way, we had better agree to say nothing at all about it in the regiment.'

"'I should think not,' Charley said. 'We should never hear the end of it; they would chaff us out of our lives.'

"We kept our secret, and came at last to laugh over it heartily when we were together. Then the subject dropped, and by the end of a year had as much escaped our minds as any other dream would have done. Three months after the affair the regiment was ordered down to Allahabad, and the change of place no doubt helped to erase all memory of the dream. Four years after we had left Jubbalpore we went to Beerapore. The time is very marked in my memory, because the very week we arrived there, your aunt, then Miss Gardiner, came out from England, to her father, our colonel. The instant I saw her I was impressed with the idea that I knew her intimately. I recollected her face, her figure, and the very tone of her voice, but wherever I had met her I could not conceive. Upon the occasion of my first introduction to her, I could not help telling her that I was convinced that we had met, and asking her if she did not remember it. No, she did not remember, but very likely she might have done so, and she suggested the names of several people at whose houses we might have met. I did not know any of them. Presently she asked how long I had been out in India?

"'Six years,' I said.

"'And how old, Mr. Harley,' she said, 'do you take me to be?'

"I saw in one instant my stupidity, and was stammering out an apology, when she went on, —

"'I am very little over eighteen, Mr. Harley, although I evidently look ever so many years older; but papa can certify to my age; so I was only twelve when you left England.'

"I tried in vain to clear matters up. Your aunt would insist that I took her to be forty, and the fun that my blunder made rather drew us together, and gave me a start over the other fellows at the station, half of whom fell straightway in love with her. Some months went on, and when the mutiny broke out we were engaged to be married. It is a proof of how completely the opium dreams had passed out of the minds of both Simmonds and myself, that even when rumours of general disaffection among the Sepoys began to be current, they never once recurred to us; and even when the news of the actual mutiny reached us, we were just as confident as were the others of the fidelity of our own regiment. It was the old story, foolish confidence and black treachery. As at very many other stations, the mutiny broke out when we were at mess. Our regiment was dining with the 34th Bengalees. Suddenly, just as dinner was over, the window was opened, and a tremendous fire poured in. Four or five men fell dead at once, and the poor colonel, who was next to me, was shot right through the head. Every one rushed to his sword and drew his pistol — for we had been ordered to carry pistols as part of our uniform. I was next to Charley Simmonds as the Sepoys of both regiments, headed by Subadar Pirán, poured in at the windows.

"'I have it now,' Charley said; 'it is the scene I dreamed.'

"As he spoke he fired his revolver at the subadar, who fell dead in his tracks.

"A Sepoy close by levelled his musket and fired. Charley fell, and the fellow rushed forward to bayonet him. As he did so I sent a bullet through his head, and he fell across Charley. It was a wild fight for a minute or two, and then a few of us made a sudden rush together, cut our way through the mutineers, and darted through an open window on to the parade. There were shouts, shots, and screams from the officers' bungalows, and in several places flames were already rising. What became of the other men I knew not, I made as hard as I could tear for the colonel's bungalow. Suddenly I came upon a sowar sitting on his horse watching the rising flames. Before he saw me I was on him, and ran him through. I leapt on his horse and galloped down to Gardiner's compound I saw lots of Sepoys in and around the bungalow, all engaged in looting. I dashed into the compound.

"'May! May!' I shouted. 'Where are you?'

"I had scarcely spoken before a dark figure rushed out of a clump of bushes close by with a scream of delight.

"In an instant she was on the horse before me, and shooting down a couple of fellows who made a rush at my reins, I dashed out again. Stray shots were fired after us. But fortunately the Sepoys were all busy looting, most of them had laid down their muskets, and no one really took up the pursuit. I turned off from the parade-ground, dashed down between the hedges of two compounds, and in another minute we were in the open country.

"Fortunately, the cavalry were all down looting their own lines, or we must have been overtaken at once. May happily had fainted as I lifted her on to my horse — happily, because the fearful screams that we heard from the various bungalows almost drove me mad, and would probably have killed her, for the poor ladies were all her intimate friends.

"I rode on for some hours, till I felt quite safe from any immediate pursuit, and then we halted in the shelter of a clump of trees.

"By this time I had heard May's story. She had felt uneasy at being alone, but had laughed at herself for being so, until upon her speaking to one of the servants he had answered in a tone of gross insolence, which had astonished her. She at once guessed that there was danger, and the moment that she was alone caught up a large, dark carriage rug, wrapped it round her so as to conceal her white dress, and stole out into the verandah. The night was dark, and scarcely had she left the house than she heard a burst of firing across at the mess-house. She at once ran in among the bushes and crouched there, as she heard the rush of men into the room she had just left. She heard them searching for her, but they were looking for a white dress, and her dark rug saved her. What she must have suffered in the five minutes between the firing of the first shots and my arrival, she only knows. May had spoken but very little since we started. I believe that she was certain that her father was dead, although I had given an evasive answer when she asked me; and her terrible sense of loss, added to the horror of that time of suspense in the garden, had completely stunned her. We waited in the tope until the afternoon, and then set out again.

"We had gone but a short distance when we saw a body of the rebel cavalry in pursuit. They had no doubt been scouring the country generally, and the discovery was accidental. For a short time we kept away from them, but this could not be for long, as our horse was carrying double. I made for a sort of ruin I saw at the foot of a hill half a mile away. I did so with no idea of the possibility of concealment. My intention was simply to get my back to a rock and to sell my life as dearly as I could, keeping the last two barrels of the revolver for ourselves. Certainly no remembrance of my dream influenced me in any way, and in the wild whirl of excitement I had not given a second thought to Charley Simmonds' exclamation. As we rode up to the ruins only a hundred yards ahead of us, May said, —

"'Blow out my brains, Edward; don't let me fall alive into their hands.'

"A shock of remembrance shot across me. The chase, her pale face, the words, the temple — all my dream rushed into my mind.

"'We are saved,' I cried, to her amazement, as we rode into the courtyard, in whose centre a great figure was sitting.

"I leapt from the horse, snatched the mussuk of water from the saddle, and then hurried May round the idol, between which and the rock behind, there was but just room to get along.

"Not a doubt entered my mind but that I should find the spring as I had dreamed. Sure enough there was the carving, fresh upon my memory as if I had seen it but the day before. I placed my hand on the leaflet without hesitation, a solid stone moved back, I hurried my amazed companion in, and shut to the stone. I found, and shot to, a massive bolt, evidently placed to prevent the door being opened by accident or design when anyone was in the idol.

"At first it seemed quite dark, but a faint light streamed in from above; we made our way up the stairs, and found that the light came through a number of small holes pierced in the upper part of the head, and through still smaller holes lower down, not much larger than a good-sized knitting-needle could pass through. These holes, we afterwards found, were in the ornaments round the idol's neck. The holes enlarged inside, and enabled us to have a view all round.

"The mutineers were furious at our disappearance, and for hours searched about. Then, saying that we must be hidden somewhere, and that they would wait till we came out, they proceeded to bivouac in the courtyard of the temple.

"We passed four terrible days, but on the morning of the fifth a scout came in to tell the rebels that a column of British troops marching on Delhi would pass close by the temple. They therefore hastily mounted and galloped off.

"Three quarters of an hour later we were safe among our own people. A fortnight afterwards your aunt and I were married. It was no time for ceremony then; there were no means of sending her away; no place where she could have waited until the time for her mourning for her father was over. So we were married quietly by one of the chaplains of the troops, and, as your storybooks say, have lived very happily ever after."

"And how about Mr. Simmonds, uncle? Did he get safe off too?"

"Yes, his dream came as vividly to his mind as mine had done. He crawled to the place where he knew the trapdoor would be, and got into the cellar. Fortunately for him there were plenty of eatables there, and he lived there in concealment for a fortnight. After that he crawled out, and found the mutineers had marched for Delhi. He went through a lot, but at last joined us before that city. We often talked over our dreams together, and there was no question that we owed our lives to them. Even then we did not talk much to other people about them, for there would have been a lot of talk, and inquiry, and questions, and you know fellows hate that sort of thing. So we held our tongues. Poor Charley's silence was sealed a year later at Lucknow, for on the advance with Lord Clyde he was killed.

"And now, boys and girls, you must run off to bed. Five minutes more and it will be Christmas day. So you see, Frank, that although I don't believe in ghosts, I have yet met with a circumstance which I cannot account for."

"It is very curious anyhow, uncle, and beats ghost stories into fits."

"I like it better, certainly," one of the girls said, "for we can go to bed without being afraid of dreaming about it."

"Well, you must not talk any more now. Off to bed, off to bed," Colonel Harley said, "or I shall get into terrible disgrace with your fathers and mothers, who have been looking very gravely at me for the last three quarters of an hour."

WHITE-FACED DICK

A STORY OF PINE-TREE GULCH

HOW Pine-tree Gulch got its name no one knew, for in the early days every ravine and hillside was thickly covered with pines. It may be that a tree of exceptional size caught the eye of the first explorer, that he camped under it, and named the place in its honour; or, may be, some fallen giant lay in the bottom and hindered the work of the first prospectors. At any rate, Pine-tree Gulch it was, and the name was as good as any other. The pine-trees were gone now. Cut up for firing, or for the erection of huts, or the construction of sluices, but the hillside was ragged with their stumps.

The principal camp was at the mouth of the Gulch, where the little stream, which scarce afforded water sufficient for the cradles in the dry season, but which was a rushing torrent in winter, joined the Yuba. The best ground was at the junction of the streams, and lay, indeed, in the Yuba valley rather than in the Gulch. At first most gold had been found higher up, but there was here comparatively little depth down to the bedrock, and as the ground became exhausted the miners moved down towards the mouth of the Gulch. They were doing well as a whole, how well no one knew, for miners are chary of giving information as to what they are making; still, it was certain they were doing well, for the bars were doing a roaring trade, and the storekeepers never refused credit — a proof in itself that the prospects were good.

The flat at the mouth of the Gulch was a busy scene, every foot was good paying stuff, for in the eddy, where the torrents in winter rushed down into the Yuba, the gold had settled down and lay thick among the gravel. But most of the parties were sinking, and it was a long way down to the bedrock; for the hills on both sides sloped steeply, and the Yuba must here at one time have rushed through a narrow gorge, until, in some wild freak, it brought down millions of tons of gravel, and resumed its course seventy feet above its former level.

A quarter of a mile higher up a ledge of rock ran across the valley, and over it in the old time the Yuba had poured in a cascade seventy feet deep into the ravine. But the rock now was level with the gravel, only showing its jagged points here and there above it. This ledge had been invaluable to the diggers: without it they could only have sunk their shafts with the greatest difficulty, for the gravel would have been full of water, and even with the greatest pains in puddling and timber-work the pumps would scarcely have sufficed to keep it down as it rose in the bottom of the shafts. But the miners had made common cause together, and giving each so many ounces of gold or so many day's work had erected a dam thirty feet high along the ledge of rock, and had cut a channel for the Yuba along the lower slopes of the valley. Of course, when the rain set in, as everybody knew, the dam would go, and the river diggings must be abandoned till the water subsided and a fresh dam was made; but there were two months before them yet, and every one hoped to be down to the bedrock before the water interrupted their work.

The hillside, both in the Yuba Valley and for some distance along Pine-tree Gulch, was dotted by shanties and tents; the former constructed for the most part of logs roughly squared, the walls being some three feet in height, on which the sharp sloping roof was placed, thatched in the first place with boughs, and made all snug, perhaps, with an old sail stretched over all. The camp was quiet enough during the day. The few women were away with their washing at the pools, a quarter of a mile up the Gulch, and the only persons to be seen about were the men told off for cooking for their respective parties.

But in the evening the camp was lively. Groups of men in red shirts and corded trousers tied at the knee, in high boots, sat round blazing fires, and talked of their prospects or discussed the news of the luck at other camps. The sound of music came from two or three plank erections which rose conspicuously above the huts of the diggers, and were bright externally with the glories of white and coloured paints. To and from these men were always sauntering, and it needed not the clink of glasses and the sound of music to tell that they were the bars of the camp.

Here, standing at the counter, or seated at numerous small tables, men were drinking villainous liquor, smoking and talking, and paying but scant attention to the strains of the fiddle or the accordion, save when some well-known air was played, when all would join in a boisterous chorus. Some were always passing in or out of a door which led into a room behind. Here there was comparative quiet, for men were gambling, and gambling high.

Going backwards and forwards with liquors into the gambling-room of the Imperial Saloon, which stood just where Pinetree Gulch opened into Yuba valley, was a lad, whose appearance had earned for him the name of White-faced Dick.

White-faced Dick was not one of those who had done well at Pine-tree Gulch; he had come across the plains with his father, who had died when half way over, and Dick had been thrown cn the world to shift for himself. Nature had not intended him for the work, for he was a delicate, timid lad; what spirits he originally had having been years before beaten out of him by a brutal father. So far, indeed, Dick was the better rather than the worse for the event which had left him an orphan.

They had been travelling with a large party for mutual security against Indians and Mormons, and so long as the journey lasted Dick had got on fairly well. He was always ready to do odd jobs, and as the draught cattle were growing weaker and weaker, and every pound of weight was of importance, no one grudged him his rations in return for his services; but when the company began to descend the slopes of the Sierra Nevada they began to break up, going off by twos and threes to the diggings, of which they heard such glowing accounts. Some, however, kept straight on to Sacramento, determining there to obtain news as to the doings at all the different places, and then to choose that which seemed to offer the best prospects of success.

Dick proceeded with them to the town, and there found himself alone. His companions were absorbed in the busy rush of population, and each had so much to provide and arrange for, that none gave a thought to the solitary boy. However, at that time no one who had a pair of hands, however feeble, to work need starve in Sacramento; and for some weeks Dick hung around the town doing odd jobs, and then, having saved a few dollars, determined to try his luck at the diggings, and started on foot with a shovel on his shoulder and a few day's provisions slung across it.

Arrived at his destination, the lad soon discovered that gold-digging was hard work for brawny and seasoned men, and after a few feeble attempts in spots abandoned as worthless he gave up the effort, and again began to drift; and even in Pine-tree Gulch it was not difficult to get a living. At first he tried rocking cradles, but the work was far harder than it appeared. He was standing ankle deep in water from morning till night, and his cheeks grew paler, and his strength, instead of increasing, seemed to fade away. Still, there were jobs within his strength. He could keep a fire alight and watch a cooking-pot, he could carry up buckets of water or wash a flannel shirt, and so he struggled on, until at last some kind-hearted man suggested to him that he should try to get a place at the new saloon which was about to be opened.

"You are not fit for this work, young 'un, and you ought to be at home with your mother; if you like I will go up with you this evening to Jeffries. I knew him down on the flats, and I daresay he will take you on. I don't say as a saloon is a good place for a boy, still you will always get your bellyful of victuals and a dry place to sleep in, if it's only under a table. What do you say?"

Dick thankfully accepted the offer, and on Red George's recommendation was that evening engaged. His work was not hard now, for till the miners knocked off there was little doing in the saloon; a few men would come in for a drink at dinnertime, but it was not until the lamps were lit that business began in earnest, and then for four or five hours Dick was busy.

A rougher or healthier lad would not have minded the work, but to Dick it was torture; every nerve in his body thrilled whenever rough miners cursed him for not carrying out their orders more quickly, or for bringing them the wrong liquors, which, as his brain was in a whirl with the noise, the shouting, and the multiplicity of orders, happened frequently. He might have fared worse had not Red George always stood his friend, and Red George was an authority in Pine-tree Gulch — powerful in frame, reckless in bearing and temper, he had been in a score of fights and had come off them, if not unscathed, at least victorious. He was notoriously a lucky digger, but his earnings went as fast as they were made, and he was always ready to open his belt and give a bountiful pinch of dust to any mate down on his luck.

One evening Dick was more helpless and confused than usual. The saloon was full, and he had been shouted at and badgered and cursed until he scarcely knew what he was doing. High play was going on in the saloon, and a good many men were clustered round the table. Red George was having a run of luck, and there was a big pile of gold dust on the table before him. One of the gamblers who was losing had ordered old rye, and instead of bringing it to him, Dick brought a tumbler of hot liquor which someone else had called for. With an oath the man took it up and threw it in his face.

"You cowardly hound!" Red George exclaimed. "Are you man enough to do that to a man?"

"You bet," the gambler, who was a new arrival at Pine-tree Gulch, replied; and picking up an empty glass, he hurled it at Red George. The bystanders sprang aside, and in a moment the two men were facing each other with outstretched pistols. The two reports rung out simultaneously: Red George sat down unconcernedly with a streak of blood flowing down his face, where the bullet had cut a furrow in his cheek; the stranger fell back with the bullet hole in the centre of his forehead.

The body was carried outside, and the play continued as if no interruption had taken place. They were accustomed to such occurrences in Pine-tree Gulch, and the piece of ground at the top of the hill, that had been set aside as a burial place, was already dotted thickly with graves, filled in almost every instance by men who had died, in the local phraseology, "with their boots on."

Neither then nor afterwards did Red George allude to the subject to Dick, whose life after this signal instance of his championship was easier than it had hitherto been, for there were few in Pine-tree Gulch who cared to excite Red George's anger; and strangers going to the place were sure to receive a friendly warning that it was best for their health to keep their tempers over any shortcomings on the part of White-faced Dick.

Grateful as he was for Red George's interference on his behalf, Dick felt the circumstance which had ensued more than anyone else in the camp. With others it was the subject of five minutes' talk, but Dick could not get out of his head the thought of the dead man's face as he fell back. He had seen many such frays before, but he was too full of his own troubles for them to make much impression upon him. But in the present case he felt as if he himself was responsible for the death of the gambler; if he had not blundered this would not have happened. He wondered whether the dead man had a wife and children, and, if so, were they expecting his return? Would they ever hear where he had died, and how?

But this feeling, which, tired out as he was when the time came for closing the bar, often prevented him from sleeping for hours, in no way lessened his gratitude and devotion towards Red George, and he felt that he could die willingly if his life would benefit his champion. Sometimes he thought, too, that his life would not be much to give, for in spite of shelter and food, the cough which he had caught while working in the water still clung to him, and, as his employer said to him angrily one day —

"Your victuals don't do you no good, Dick; you get thinner and thinner, and folks will think as I starve you. Darned if you ain't a disgrace to the establishment."

The wind was whistling down the gorges, and the clouds hung among the pine-woods which still clothed the upper slopes of the hills, and the diggers, as they turned out one morning, looked up apprehensively.

"But it could not be," they assured each other. Every one knew that the rains were not due for another month yet; it could only be a passing shower if it rained at all.

But as the morning went on, men came in from camps higher up the river, and reports were current that it had been raining for the last two days among the upper hills; while those who took the trouble to walk across to the new channel could see for themselves at noon that it was filled very nigh to the brim, the water rushing along with thick and turbid current. But those who repeated the rumours, or who reported that the channel was full, were summarily put down. Men would not believe that such a calamity as a flood and the destruction of all their season's work could be impending. There had been some showers, no doubt, as there had often been before, but it was ridiculous to talk of anything like rain a month before its time. Still, in spite of these assertions, there was uneasiness at Pine-tree Gulch, and men looked at the driving clouds above and shook their heads before they went down to the shafts to work after dinner.

When the last customer had left and the bar was closed, Dick had nothing to do till evening, and he wandered outside and sat down on a stump, at first looking at the work going on in the valley, then so absorbed in his own thoughts that he noticed nothing, not even the driving mist which presently set in. He was calculating that he had, with his savings from his wages and what had been given him by the miners, laid by eighty dollars. When he got another hundred and twenty he would go; he would make his way down to San Francisco, and then by ship to Panama and up to New York, and then west again to the village where he was born. There would be people there who would know him, and who would give him work, for his mother's sake. He did not care what it was; anything would be better than this.

Then his thoughts came back to Pine-tree Gulch, and he started to his feet. Could he be mistaken? Were his eyes deceiving him? No; among the stones and boulders of the old bed of the Yuba there was the gleam of water, and even as he watched it he could see it widening out. He started to run down the hill to give the alarm, but before he was halfway he paused, for there were loud shouts, and a scene of bustle and confusion instantly arose.

The cradles were deserted, and the men working on the surface loaded themselves with their tools and made for the high ground, while those at the windlasses worked their hardest to draw up their comrades below. A man coming down from above stopped close to Dick, with a low cry, and stood gazing with a white scared face. Dick had worked with him; he was one of the company to which Red George belonged.

"What is it, Saunders?"

"My God! they are lost," the man replied. "I was at the windlass when they shouted up to me to go up and fetch them a bottle of rum. They had just struck it rich, and wanted a drink on the strength of it."

Dick understood at once. Red George and his mates were still in the bottom of the shaft, ignorant of the danger which was threatening them.

"Come on," he cried; "we shall be in time yet," and at the top of his speed dashed down the hill, followed by Saunders.

"What is it, what is it?" asked parties of men mounting the hill. "Red George's gang are still below."

Dick's eyes were fixed on the water. There was a broad band now of yellow with a white edge down the centre of the stony flat, and it was widening with terrible rapidity. It was scarce ten yards from the windlass at the top of Red George's shaft when Dick, followed closely by Saunders, reached it.

"Come up, mates; quick, for your lives! The river is rising; you will be flooded out directly. Every one else has gone!"

As he spoke he pulled at the rope by which the bucket was hanging, and the handles of the windlass flew round rapidly as it descended. When it had run out, Dick and he grasped the handles.

"All right below?"

An answering call came up, and the two began their work, throwing their whole strength into it. Quickly as the windlass revolved, it seemed an endless time to Dick before the bucket came up, and the first man stepped out. It was not Red George. Dick had hardly expected it would be. Red George would be sure to see his two mates up before him, and the man uttered a cry of alarm as he saw the water, now within a few feet of the mouth of the shaft.

It was a torrent now, for not only was it coming through the dam, but it was rushing down in cascades from the new channel. Without a word the miner placed himself facing Dick and the moment the bucket was again down, the three grasped the handles. But quickly as they worked, the edge of the water was within a few inches of the shaft when the next man reached the surface; but again the bucket descended before the rope tightened. However, the water had began to run over the lip — at first in a mere trickle, and then, almost instantaneously, in a cascade, which grew larger and larger.

The bucket was halfway up when a sound like thunder was heard, the ground seemed to tremble under their feet, and then at the turn of the valley above, a great wave of yellow water, crested with foam, was seen tearing along at the speed of a racehorse.

"The dam has burst!" Saunders shouted. "Run for your lives, or we are all lost!"

The three men dropped the handles and ran at full speed towards the shore, while loud shouts to Dick to follow came from the crowd of men standing on the slope. But the boy still grasped the handles, and with lips tightly closed, still toiled on. Slowly the bucket ascended, for Red George was a heavy man; then suddenly the weight slackened, and the handle went round faster. The shaft was filling, the water had reached the bucket, and had risen to Red

George's neck, so that his weight was no longer on the rope. So fast did the water pour in, that it was not half a minute before the bucket reached the surface, and Red George sprang out. There was but time for one exclamation, and then the great wave struck them. Red George was whirled like a straw in the current; but he was a strong swimmer, and at a point where the valley widened out, half a mile lower, he struggled to shore.

Two days later the news reached Pine-tree Gulch that a boy's body had been washed ashore twenty miles down, and ten men, headed by Red George, went and brought it solemnly back to Pine-tree Gulch. There, among the stumps of pine-trees, a grave was dug, and there, in the presence of the whole camp, White-faced Dick was laid to rest.

Pine-tree Gulch is a solitude now, the trees are growing again, and none would dream that it was once a busy scene of industry; but if the traveller searches among the pine-trees, he will find a stone with the words:

"Here lies White-faced Dick, who died to save Red George. 'What can a man do more than give his life for a friend?'"

The text was the suggestion of an ex-clergyman working as a miner in Pine-tree Gulch.

Red George worked no more at the diggings, but after seeing the stone laid in its place, went east, and with what little money came to him when the common fund of the company was divided after the flood on the Yuba, bought a small farm, and settled down there; but to the end of his life he was never weary of telling those who would listen to it the story of Pine-tree Gulch.

A BRUSH WITH
THE CHINESE

AND WHAT CAME OF IT

IT was early in December that H.M.S. *Perseus* was cruising off the mouth of the Canton River. War had been declared with China in consequence of her continued evasions of the treaty she had made with us, and it was expected that a strong naval force would soon gather to bring her to reason. In the meantime the ships on the station had a busy time of it, chasing the enemy's junks when they ventured to show themselves beyond the reach of the guns of their forts, and occasionally having a brush with the piratical boats which took advantage of the general confusion to plunder friend as well as foe.

The *Perseus* had that afternoon chased two Government junks up a creek. The sun had already set when they took refuge there, and the captain did not care to send his boats after them in the dark, as many of the creeks ran up for miles into the flat country; and as they not unfrequently had many arms or branches, the boats might, in the dark, miss the junks altogether. Orders were issued that four boats should be ready for starting at daybreak the next morning. The *Perseus* anchored off the mouth of the creek, and two boats were ordered to row backwards and forwards off its mouth all night to insure that the enemy did not slip out in the darkness.

Jack Fothergill, the senior midshipman, was commanding the gig, and two of the other midshipmen were going in the pinnace and launch, commanded respectively by the first lieutenant and the master. The three other midshipmen of the *Perseus* were loud in their lamentations that they were not to take share in the fun.

"You can't all go, you know," Fothergill said, "and it's no use making a row about it; the captain has been very good to let three of us go."

"It's all very well for you, Jack," Percy Adcock, the youngest of the lads, replied, "because you are one of those chosen; and it is not so hard for Simmons and Linthorpe, because they went the other day in the boat that chased those junks under shelter of the guns of their battery, but I haven't had a chance for ever so long."

"What fun was there in chasing the junks?" Simmons said. "We never got near the brutes till they were close to their battery, and then just as the first shot came singing from their guns, and we thought that we were going to have some excitement, the first lieutenant sung out 'Easy all,' and there was nothing for it but to turn round and to row for the ship, and a nice hot row it was — two hours and a half in a broiling sun. Of course I am not blaming Oliphant, for the captain's orders were strict that we were not to try to cut the junks out if they got under the guns of any of their batteries. Still it was horribly annoying, and I do think the captain might have remembered what beastly luck we had last time, and given us a chance tomorrow."

"It is clear we could not all go," Fothergill said, "and naturally enough the captain chose the three seniors. Besides, if you did have bad luck last time, you had your chance, and I don't suppose we shall have anything more exciting now; these fellows always set fire to their junks and row for the shore directly they see us, after firing a shot or two wildly in our direction."

"Well, Jack, if you don't expect any fun," Simmons replied, "perhaps you wouldn't mind telling the first lieutenant you do not care for going, and that I am very anxious to take your place. Perhaps he will be good enough to allow me to relieve you."

"A likely thing that!" Fothergill laughed. "No, Tom, I am sorry you are not going, but you must make the best of it till another chance comes."

"Don't you think, Jack," Percy Adcock said to his senior in a coaxing tone later on, "you could manage to smuggle me into the boat with you?"

"Not I, Percy. Suppose you got hurt, what would the captain say then? And firing as wildly as the Chinese do, a shot is just as likely to hit your little carcase as to lodge in one of the sailors. No, you must just make the best of it, Percy, and I promise you that next time there is a boat expedition, if you are not put in, I will say a good word to the first luff for you."

"That promise is better than nothing," the boy said; "but I would a deal rather go this time and take my chance next."

"But you see you can't, Percy, and there's no use talking any more about it. I really do not expect there will be any fighting. Two junks would hardly make any opposition to the boats of the ship, and I expect we shall be back by nine o'clock with the news that they were well on fire before we came up."

Percy Adcock, however, was determined, if possible, to go. He was a favourite among the men, and when he spoke to the bow oar of the gig, the latter promised to do anything he could to aid him to carry out his wishes.

"We are to start at daybreak, Tom, so that it will be quite dark when the boats are lowered. I will creep into the gig before that and hide myself as well as I can under your thwart, and all you have got to do is to take no notice of me. When the boat is lowered I think they will hardly make me out from the deck, especially as you will be standing up in the bow holding on with the boat-hook till the rest get on board."

"Well, sir, I will do my best; but if you are caught you must not let out that I knew anything about it."

"I won't do that," Percy said. "I don't think there is much chance of my being noticed until we get on board the junks, and then they won't know which boat I came off in, and the first lieutenant will be too busy to blow me up. Of course I shall get it when I am on board again, but I don't mind that so that I see the fun. Besides, I want to send home some things to my sister, and she will like them all the better if I can tell her I captured them on board some junks we seized and burnt."

The next morning the crews mustered before daybreak. Percy had already taken his place under the bow thwart of the gig. The davits were swung overboard, and two men took their places in her as she was lowered down by the falls. As soon as she touched the water the rest of the crew clambered down by the ladder and took their places; then Fothergill took his seat in the stern, and the boat pushed off and lay a few lengths away from the ship until the heavier boats put off. As soon as they were under way Percy crawled out from his hiding-place and placed himself in the bow, where he was sheltered by the body of the oarsmen from Fothergill's sight.

Day was just breaking now, but it was still dark on the water, and the boat rowed very slowly until it became lighter. Percy could just make out the shores of the creek on both sides; they were but two or three feet above the level of the water, and were evidently submerged at high tide. The creek was about a hundred yards wide, and the lad could not see far ahead, for it was full of sharp windings and turnings. Here and there branches joined it, but the boats were evidently following the main channel. After another half hour's rowing the first lieutenant suddenly gave the order, "Easy all," and the men, looking over their shoulders, saw a village a quarter of a mile ahead, with the two junks they had chased the night before lying in front of it. Almost at the same moment a sudden uproar was heard — drums were beaten and gongs sounded.

"They are on the lookout for us," the first lieutenant said. "Mr. Mason, do you keep with me and attack the junk highest up the river; Mr. Bellew and Mr. Fothergill, do you take the one lower down. Row on, men."

The oars all touched the water together, and the four boats leapt forward. In a minute a scattering fire of gingals and matchlocks was opened from the junks, and the bullets pattered on the water round the boats. Percy was kneeling up in the bow now. As they passed a branch channel three or four hundred yards from the village, he started and leapt to his feet.

"There are four or five junks in that passage, Fothergill; they are poling out."

The first lieutenant heard the words.

"Row on, men; let us finish with these craft ahead before the others get out. This must be that piratical village we have heard about, Mr. Mason, as lying up one of these creeks; that accounts for those two junks not going higher up. I was surprised at seeing them here, for they might guess that we should try to get them this morning. Evidently they calculated on catching us in a trap."

Percy was delighted at finding that, in the excitement caused by his news, the first lieutenant had forgotten to take any notice of his being there without orders, and he returned a defiant nod to the threat conveyed by Fothergill shaking his fist at him. As they neared the junks the fire of those on board redoubled, and was aided by that of many villagers gathered on the bank of the creek. Suddenly from a bank of rushes four cannons were fired. A ball struck the pinnace, smashing in her side. The other boats gathered hastily round and took her crew on board, and then dashed at the junks, which were but a hundred yards distant. The valour of the Chinese evaporated as they saw the boats approaching, and scores of them leapt overboard and swam for shore.

In another minute the boats were alongside and the crews scrambling up the sides of the junks. A few Chinamen only attempted to oppose them. These were speedily overcome, and the British had now time to look round, and saw that six junks crowded with men had issued from the side creek and were making towards them.

"Let the boats tow astern," the lieutenant ordered. "We should have to run the gauntlet of that battery on shore if we were to attack them, and might lose another boat before we reached their side. We will fight them here."

The junks approached, those on board firing their guns, yelling and shouting, while the drums and gongs were furiously beaten.

"They will find themselves mistaken, Percy, if they think they are going to frighten us with all that row," Fothergill said. "You young rascal, how did you get on board the boat without being seen? The captain will be sure to suspect I had a hand in concealing you."

The tars were now at work firing the gingals attached to the bulwarks and the matchlocks, with which the deck was strewn, at the approaching junks. As they took steady aim, leaning their pieces on the bulwarks, they did considerable execution among the Chinamen crowded on board the junks, while the shot of the Chinese, for the most part, whistled far overhead; but the guns of the shore battery, which had now been slewed round to bear upon them, opened with a better aim, and several shots came crashing into the sides of the two captured junks.

"Get ready to board, lads!" Lieutenant Oliphant shouted. "Don't wait for them to board you, but the moment they come alongside lash their rigging to ours and spring on board them."

The leading junk was now about twenty yards away, and presently grated alongside. Half-a-dozen sailors at once sprang into her rigging with ropes, and after lashing the junks together leaped down upon her deck, where Fothergill was leading the gig's crew and some of those rescued from the pinnace, while Mr. Bellew, with another party, had boarded her at the stern. Several of the

Chinese fought stoutly, but the greater part lost heart at seeing themselves attacked by the "white devils," instead of, as they expected, overwhelming them by their superior numbers. Many began at once to jump overboard, and after two or three minutes' sharp fighting, the rest either followed their example or were beaten below.

Fothergill looked round. The other junk had been attacked by two of the enemy, one on each side, and the little body of sailors were gathered in her waist, and were defending themselves against an overwhelming number of the enemy.

The other three piratical junks had been carried somewhat up the creek by the tide that was sweeping inward, and could not for the moment take part in the fight.

"Mr. Oliphant is hard pressed, sir." He asked the master: "Shall we take to the boats?"

"That will be the best plan," Mr. Bellew replied. "Quick, lads, get the boats alongside and tumble in; there is not a moment to be lost."

The crew at once sprang to the boats and rowed to the other junk, which was but some thirty yards away.

The Chinese, absorbed in their contest with the crew of the pinnace, did not perceive the newcomers until they gained the deck, and with a shout fell furiously upon them. In their surprise and consternation the pirates did not pause to note that they were still five to one superior in number, but made a precipitate rush for their own vessels. The English at once took the offensive. The first lieutenant with his party boarded one, while the newcomers leapt on to the deck of the other. The panic which had seized the Chinese was so complete that they attempted no resistance whatever, but sprang overboard in great numbers and swam to the shore, which was but twenty yards away, and in three minutes the English were in undisputed possession of both vessels.

"Back again, Mr. Fothergill, or you will lose the craft you captured," Lieutenant Oliphant said; "they have already cut her free."

The Chinese, indeed, who had been beaten below by the boarding party, had soon perceived the sudden departure of their captors, and gaining the deck again had cut the lashings which fastened them to the other junk, and were proceeding to hoist their sails. They were too late, however. Almost before the craft had way on her Fothergill and his crew were alongside. The Chinese did not wait for the attack, but at once sprang overboard and made for the shore. The other three junks, seeing the capture of their comrades, had already hoisted their sails and were making up the creek. Fothergill dropped an anchor, left four of his men in charge, and rowed back to Mr. Oliphant.

"What shall we do next, sir?"

"We will give those fellows on shore a lesson, and silence their battery. Two men have been killed since you left. We must let the other junks go for the present. Four of my men were killed and eleven wounded before Mr. Bellew and you came to our assistance. The Chinese were fighting pluckily up to that time, and it would have gone very hard with us if you had not been at hand; the beggars will fight when they think they have got it all their own way. But before we land we will set fire to the five junks we have taken. Do you return and see that the two astern are well lighted, Mr. Fothergill; Mr. Mason will see to these three. When you have done your work take to your boat and lay off till I join you; keep the junks between you and the shore, to protect you from the fire of the rascals there."

"I cannot come with you, I suppose, Fothergill?" Percy Adcock said, as the midshipman was about to descend into his boat again.

"Yes, come along, Percy. It doesn't matter what you do now. The captain will be so pleased when he hears that we have captured and burnt five junks, that you will get off with a very light wigging, I imagine."

"That's just what I was thinking, Jack. Has it not been fun?"

"You wouldn't have thought it fun if you had got one of those matchlock balls in your body. There are a good many of our poor fellows just at the present moment who do not see anything funny in the affair at all. Here we are; clamber up."

The crew soon set to work under Fothergill's orders. The sails were cut off the masts and thrown down into the hold; bamboos, of which there were an abundance down there, were heaped over them, a barrel of oil was poured over the mass, and the fire then applied.

"That will do, lads. Now take to your boats and let's make a bonfire of the other junk."

In ten minutes both vessels were a sheet of flame, and the boat was lying a short distance from them waiting for further operations. The inhabitants of the village, furious at the failure of the plan which had been laid for the destruction of the "white devils," kept up a constant fusilade, which, however, did no harm, for the gig was completely sheltered by the burning junks close to her from their missiles.

"There go the others!" Percy exclaimed after a minute or two, as three columns of smoke arose simultaneously from the other junks, and the sailors were seen dropping into their boats alongside.

The killed and wounded were placed in the other gig with four sailors in charge. They were directed to keep under shelter of the junks until rejoined by the pinnace and Fothergill's gig, after these had done their work on shore.

When all was ready the first lieutenant raised his hand as a signal, and the two boats dashed between the burning junks and rowed for the shore. Such of the natives as had their weapons charged fired a hasty volley, and then, as the sailors leapt from their boats, took to their heels.

"Mr. Fothergill, take your party into the village and set fire to the houses; shoot down every man you see. This place is a nest of pirates. I will capture that battery and then join you."

Fothergill and his sailors at once entered the village. The men had already fled; the women were turned out of the houses, and these were immediately set on fire. The tars regarded the whole affair as a glorious joke, and raced from house to house, making a hasty search in each for concealed valuables before setting it on fire. In a short time the whole village was in a blaze.

"There is a house there, standing in that little grove a hundred yards away," Percy said.

"It looks like a temple," Fothergill replied. "However, we will have a look at it." And calling two sailors to accompany him, he started at a run towards it, Percy keeping by his side.

"It is a temple," Fothergill said when they approached it. "Still, we will have a look at it, but we won't burn it; it will be as well to respect the religion, even of a set of piratical scoundrels like these."

At the head of his men he rushed in at the entrance. There was a blaze of fire as half a dozen muskets were discharged in their faces. One of the sailors dropped dead, and before the others had time to realize what had happened they were beaten to the ground by a storm of blows from swords and other weapons.

A heavy blow crashed down on Percy's head, and he fell insensible even before he realized what had occurred.

When he recovered, his first sensation was that of a vague wonder as to what had happened to him. He seemed to be in darkness and unable to move hand or foot. He was compressed in some way that he could not at first understand, and was being bumped and jolted in an extraordinary manner. It was some little time before he could understand the situation. He first remembered the fight with the junks, then he recalled the landing and burning the village; then, as his brain cleared, came the recollection of his start with Fothergill for the temple among the trees, his arrival there, and a loud report and flash of fire.

"I must have been knocked down and stunned," he said to himself, "and I suppose I am a prisoner now to these brutes, and one of them must be carrying me on his back."

Yes, he could understand it all now. His hands and his feet were tied, ropes were passed round his body in every direction, and he was fastened back to back upon the shoulders of a Chinaman. Percy remembered the tales he had heard of the imprisonment and torture of those who fell into the hands of the Chinese, and he bitterly regretted that he had not been killed instead of stunned in the surprise of the temple.

"It would have been just the same feeling," he said to himself, "and there would have been an end of it. Now, there is no saying what is going to happen. I wonder whether Jack was killed, and the sailors."

Presently there was a jabber of voices; the motion ceased. Percy could feel that the cords were being unwound, and he was dropped on to his feet; then the cloth was removed from his head, and he could look round.

A dozen Chinese, armed with matchlocks and bristling with swords and daggers, stood around, and among them, bound like himself and gagged by a piece of bamboo forced lengthways across his mouth and kept there with a string going round the back of the head, stood Fothergill. He was bleeding from several cuts in the head. Percy's heart gave a bound of joy at finding that he was not alone; then he tried to feel sorry that Jack had not escaped, but failed to do so, although he told himself that his comrade's presence would not in any way alleviate the fate which was certain to befall him. Still the thought of companionship, even in wretchedness, and perhaps a vague hope that Jack, with his energy and spirit, might contrive some way for their escape, cheered him up

As Percy, too, was gagged, no word could be exchanged by the midshipmen, but they nodded to each other. They were now put side by side and made to walk in the centre of their captors. On the way they passed through several villages, whose inhabitants poured out to gaze at the captives, but the men in charge of them were evidently not disposed to delay, as they passed through without a stop. At last they halted before two cottages standing by themselves, thrust the prisoners into a small room, removed their gags, and left them to themselves.

"Well, Percy, my boy, so they caught you too? I am awfully sorry. It was my fault for going with only two men into that temple, but as the village had been deserted and scarcely a man was found there, it never entered my mind that there might be a party in the temple."

"Of course not, Jack; it was a surprise altogether. I don't know anything about it, for I was knocked down, I suppose, just as we went in, and the first thing I knew about it was that I was being carried on the back of one of those fellows. I thought it was awful at first, but I don't seem to mind so much now you are with me."

"It is a comfort to have someone to speak to," Jack said, "yet I wish you were not here, Percy; I can't do you any good, and I shall never cease blaming myself for having brought you into this scrape. I don't know much more about the affair than you do. The guns were fired so close to us that my face was scorched with one of them, and almost at the same instant I got a lick across my cheek with a sword. I had just time to hit at one of them, and then almost at the same moment I got two or three other blows, and down I went; they threw themselves on the top of me and tied and gagged me in no time. Then I was tied to a long bamboo, and two fellows put the ends on their shoulders and went off with me through the fields. Of course I was face downwards, and did not know you were with us till they stopped and loosed me from the bamboo and set me on my feet."

"But what are they going to do with us do you think, Jack?"

"I should say they are going to take us to Canton and claim a reward for our capture, and there I suppose they will cut off our heads or saw us in two, or put us to some other unpleasant kind of death. I expect they are discussing it now; do you hear what a jabber they are kicking up?"

Voices were indeed heard raised in angry altercation in the next room. After a time the din subsided and the conversation appeared to take a more amiable turn.

"I suppose they have settled it as far as they are concerned," Jack said; "anyhow, you may be quite sure they mean to make something out of us. If they hadn't they would have finished us at once, for they must have been furious at the destruction of their junks and village. As to the idea that mercy has anything to do with it, we may as well put it out of our minds. The Chinaman, at the best of times, has no feeling of pity in his nature, and after their defeat it is certain they would have killed us at once had they not hoped to do better by us. If they had been Indians I should have said they had carried us off to enjoy the satisfaction of torturing us, but I don't suppose it is that with them."

"Do you think there is any chance of our getting away?" Percy asked, after a pause.

"I should say not the least in the world, Percy. My hands are fastened so tight now that the ropes seem cutting into my wrists, and after they had set me on my feet and cut the cords of my legs I could scarcely stand at first, my feet were so numbed by the pressure. However, we must keep up our pluck. Possibly they may keep us at Canton for a bit, and if they do the squadron may arrive and fight its way past the forts and take the city before they have quite made up their minds as to what kind of death will be most appropriate to the occasion. I wonder what they are doing now? They seem to be chopping sticks."

"I wish they would give us some water," Percy said. "I am frightfully thirsty."

"And so am I, Percy; there is one comfort, they won't let us die of thirst, they could get no satisfaction out of our deaths now."

Two hours later some of the Chinese re-entered the room and

led the captives outside, and the lads then saw what was the meaning of the noise they had heard. A cage had been manufactured of strong bamboos. It was about four and a half feet long, four feet wide, and less than three feet high; above it was fastened two long bamboos. Two or three of the bars of the cage had been left open.

"My goodness! they never intend to put us in there," Percy exclaimed.

"That they do," Jack said. "They are going to carry us the rest of the way."

The cords which bound the prisoners' hands were now cut, and they were motioned to crawl into the cage. This they did; the bars were then put in their places and securely lashed. Four men went to the ends of the poles and lifted the cage upon their shoulders; two others took their places beside it, and one man, apparently the leader of the party, walked on ahead; the rest remained behind.

"I never quite realized what a fowl felt in a coop before," Jack said, "but if its sensations are at all like mine they must be decidedly unpleasant. It isn't high enough to sit upright in, it is nothing like long enough to lie down, and as to getting out one might as well think of flying. Do you know, Percy, I don't think they mean taking us to Canton at all. I did not think of it before, but from the direction of the sun I feel sure that we cannot have been going that way. What they are up to I can't imagine."

In an hour they came to a large village. Here the cage was set down and the villagers closed round. They were, however, kept a short distance from the cage by the men in charge of it. Then a wooden platter was placed on the ground, and persons throwing a few copper coins into this were allowed to come near the cage.

"They are making a show of us!" Fothergill exclaimed. "That's what they are up to, you see if it isn't; they are going to travel up country to show the 'white devils' whom their valour has captured."

This was, indeed, the purpose of the pirates. At that time Europeans seldom ventured beyond the limits assigned to them in the two or three towns where they were permitted to trade, and few, indeed, of the country people had ever obtained a sight of the white barbarians of whose doings they had so frequently heard.

Consequently a small crowd soon gathered round the cage, eyeing the captives with the same interest they would have felt as to unknown and dangerous beasts; they laughed and joked, passed remarks upon them, and even poked them with sticks. Fothergill, furious at this treatment, caught one of the sticks, and wrenching it from the hands of the Chinaman, tried to strike at him through the bars, a proceeding which excited shouts of laughter from the bystanders.

"I think, Jack," Percy said, "it will be best to try and keep our tempers and not to seem to mind what they do to us, then if they find they can't get any fun out of us they will soon leave us alone."

"Of course, that's the best plan," Fothergill agreed, "but it's not so easy to follow. That fellow very nearly poked out my eye with his stick, and no one's going to stand that if he can help it."

It was some hours before the curiosity of the village was satisfied. When all had paid who were likely to do so, the guards broke up their circle, and leaving two of their number at the cage to see that no actual harm was caused to their prisoners, the rest went off to a refreshment house. The place of the elders was now taken by the boys and children of the village, who crowded round the cage, prodded the prisoners with sticks, and, putting their hands through the bars, pulled their ears and hair. This amusement, however, was brought to an abrupt conclusion by Fothergill suddenly seizing the wrist of a big boy and pulling his arm through the cage until his face was against the bars; then he proceeded to punch him until the guard, coming to his rescue, poked Fothergill with his stick until he released his hold.

The punishment of their comrade excited neither anger nor resentment among the other boys, who yelled with delight at his discomfiture, but it made them more careful in approaching the cage, and though they continued to poke the prisoners with sticks they did not venture again to thrust a hand through the bars. At sunset the guards again came round, lifted the cage and carried it into a shed. A platter of dirty rice and a jug of water were put into the cage; two of the men lighted their long pipes and sat down on guard beside it, and, the doors being closed, the captives were left in peace.

"If this sort of thing is to go on, as I suppose it is," Fothergill said, "the sooner they cut off our heads the better."

"It is very bad, Jack. I am sore all over with those probes from their sharp sticks."

"I don't care for the pain, Percy, so much as the humiliation of the thing. To be stared at and poked at as if we were wild beasts by these curs, when with half a dozen of our men we could send a hundred of them scampering, I feel as if I could choke with rage."

"You had better try and eat some of this rice, Jack. It is beastly, but I daresay we shall get no more until tomorrow night, and we must keep up our strength if we can. At any rate, the water is not bad, that's a comfort."

"No thanks to them," Jack growled. "If there had been any bad water in the neighbourhood they would have given it to us."

For six weeks the sufferings of the prisoners continued. Their captors avoided towns where the authorities would probably at once have taken the prisoners out of their hands. No one would have recognized the two captives as the midshipmen of the *Perseus*; their clothes were in rags — torn to pieces by the thrusts of the sharp-pointed bamboos, to which they had daily been subjected — the bad food, the cramped position, and the misery which they suffered had worn both lads to skeletons; their hair was matted with filth, their faces begrimed with dirt. Percy was so weak that he felt he could not stand. Fothergill, being three years older, was less exhausted, but he knew that he, too, could not support his sufferings for many days longer. Their bodies were covered with sores, and try as they would they were able to catch only a few minutes' sleep at a time, so much did the bamboo bars hurt their wasted limbs.

They seldom exchanged a word during the daytime, suffering in silence the persecutions to which they were exposed, but at night they talked over their homes and friends in England, and their comrades on board ship, seldom saying a word as to their present position. They were now in a hilly country, but had not the least idea of the direction in which it lay from Canton or its distance from the coast.

One evening Jack said to his companion, "I think it's nearly all over now, Percy. The last two days we have made longer journeys, and have not stopped at any of the smaller villages we passed through. I fancy our guards must see that we can't last much longer, and are taking us down to some town to hand us over to the authorities and get their reward for us."

"I hope it is so, Jack; the sooner the better. Not that it makes much difference now to me, for I do not think I can stand many more days of it."

"I am afraid I am tougher than you, Percy, and shall take longer to kill, so I hope with all my heart that I may be right, and that they may be going to give us up to the authorities."

The next evening they stopped at a large place, and were subjected to the usual persecution; this, however, was now less prolonged than during the early days of their captivity, for they had now no longer strength or spirits to resent their treatment, and as no fun was to be obtained from passive victims, even the village boys soon ceased to find any amusement in tormenting them.

When most of their visitors had left them, an elderly Chinaman approached the side of the cage. He spoke to their guards and looked at them attentively for some minutes, then he said in pigeon English, "You officer men?"

"Yes!" Jack exclaimed, starting at the sound of the English words, the first they had heard spoken since their captivity. "Yes, we are officers of the *Perseus*."

"Me speeke English velly well," the Chinaman said; "me pilot-man many years on Canton river. How you get here?"

"We were attacking some piratical junks, and landed to destroy the village where the people were firing on us. We entered a place full of pirates, and were knocked down and taken prisoners, and carried away up the country; that is six weeks ago, and you see what we are now."

"Pirate men velly bad," the Chinaman said; "plunder many junk on river and kill crew. Me muchee hate them."

"Can you do anything for us?" Jack asked. "You will be well rewarded if you could manage to get us free."

The man shook his head.

"Me no see what can do, me stranger here; come to stay with wifey; people no do what me ask them. English ships attack Canton, much fight and take town, people all hate English. Bad country dis. People in one village fight against another. Velly bad men here."

"How far is Canton away?" Jack asked. "Could you not send down to tell the English we are here?"

"Fourteen days' journey off," the man said; "no see how can do anything."

"Well," Jack said, "when you get back again to Canton let our people know what has been the end of us; we shall not last much longer."

"All light," the man said, "will see what me can do. Muchee think tonight!" And after saying a few words to the guards, who had been regarding this conversation with an air of surprise, the Chinaman retired.

The guards had for some time abandoned the precaution of sitting up at night by the cage, convinced that their captives had no longer strength to attempt to break through its fastenings or to drag themselves many yards away if they could do so. They therefore left it standing in the open, and, wrapping themselves in their thickly-wadded coats, for the nights were cold, lay down by the side of the cage.

The coolness of the nights had, indeed, assisted to keep the two prisoners alive. During the day the sun was excessively hot, and the crowd of visitors round the cage impeded the circulation of the air and added to their sufferings. It was true that the cold at night frequently prevented them from sleeping, but it acted as a tonic and braced them up.

"What did he mean about the villages attacking each other?" Percy asked.

"I have heard," Jack replied, "that in some parts of China things are very much the same as they used to be in the highlands of Scotland. There is no law or order. The different villages are like clans, and wage war on each other. Sometimes the Government sends a number of troops, who put the thing down for a time, chop off a good many heads, and then march away, and the whole work begins again as soon as their backs are turned."

That night the uneasy slumber of the lads was disturbed by a sudden firing; shouts and yells were heard, and the firing redoubled.

"The village is attacked," Jack said. "I noticed that, like some other places we have come into lately, there is a strong earthen wall round it, with gates. Well, there is one comfort — it does not make much difference to us which side wins."

The guards at the first alarm leapt to their feet, caught up their matchlocks, and ran to aid in the defence of the wall. Two minutes later a man ran up to the cage.

"All lightee," he said; "just what me hopee."

With his knife he cut the tough withes that held the bamboos in their places, and pulled out three of the bars.

"Come along," he said; "no time to lose."

Jack scrambled out, but in trying to stand upright gave a sharp exclamation of pain. Percy crawled out more slowly; he tried to stand up, but could not. The Chinaman caught him up and threw him on his shoulder.

"Come along quickee," he said to Jack; "if takee village, kill evely one." He set off at a run. Jack followed as fast as he could, groaning at every step from the pain the movement caused to his bruised body.

They went to the side of the village opposite to that at which the attack was going on. They met no one on the way, the inhabitants having all rushed to the other side to repel the attack. They stopped at a small gate in the wall, the Chinaman drew back the bolts and opened it, and they passed out into the country. For an hour they kept on. By the end of that time Jack could scarcely drag his limbs along. The Chinaman halted at length in a clump of trees surrounded by a thick undergrowth.

"Allee safee here," he said, "no searchee so far; here food;" and he produced from a wallet a cold chicken and some boiled rice, and unslung from his shoulder a gourd filled with cold tea.

"Me go back now, see what happen. Tomollow nightee come again — bringee more food." And without another word went off at a rapid pace.

Jack moistened his lips with the tea, and then turned to his companion. Percy had not spoken a word since he had been released from the cage, and had been insensible during the greater part of his journey. Jack poured some cold tea between his lips.

"Cheer up, Percy, old boy, we are free now, and with luck and that good fellow's help we will work our way down to Canton yet."

"I shall never get down there; you may," Percy said feebly.

"Oh, nonsense, you will pick up strength like a steam-engine now. Here, let me prop you against this tree. That's better. Now drink a drop of this tea; it's like nectar after that filthy water we have been drinking. Now you will feel better. Now you must try and eat a little of this chicken and rice. Oh, nonsense, you have got to do it. I am not going to let you give way when our trouble is just over. Think of your people at home, Percy, and make an effort, for their sakes. Good heavens! now I think of it, it must be Christmas morning. We were caught on the 2nd and we have been just twenty-two days on show. I am sure that it must be past twelve o'clock, and it is Christmas day. It is a good omen, Percy. This food isn't like roast beef and plum-pudding, but it's not to be despised, I can tell you. Come, fire away, that's a good fellow."

Percy made an effort and ate a few mouthfuls of rice and chicken, then he took another draught of tea, and lay down, and was almost immediately asleep.

Jack ate his food slowly and contentedly till he finished half the supply, then he, too, lay down, and, after a short but hearty thanksgiving for his escape from a slow and lingering death, he, too, fell off to sleep. The sun was rising when he woke, being aroused by a slight movement on the part of Percy; he opened his eyes and sat up.

"Well, Percy, how do you feel this morning?" he asked cheerily.

"I feel too weak to move," Percy replied languidly.

"Oh, you will be all right when you have sat up and eaten breakfast," Jack said. "Here you are; here is a wing for you, and this rice is as white as snow, and the tea is first rate. I thought last night after I lay down that I heard a murmur of water, so after we have had breakfast I will look about and see if I can find it. We should feel like new men after a wash. You look awful, and I am sure I am just as bad."

The thought of a wash inspirited Percy far more than that of eating, and he sat up and made a great effort to do justice to break-fast. He succeeded much better than he had done the night before, and Jack, although he pretended to grumble, was satisfied with his companion's progress, and finished off the rest of the food. Then he set out to search for water. He had not very far to go; a tiny stream, a few inches wide and two or three inches deep, ran through the wood from the higher ground. After throwing himself down and taking a drink, he hurried back to Percy.

"It is all right, Percy, I have found it. We can wash to our hearts' content; think of that, lad."

Percy could hardly stand, but he made an effort, and Jack half carried him to the streamlet. There the lads spent hours. First they bathed their heads and hands, and then, stripping, lay down in the stream and allowed it to flow over them, then they rubbed themselves with handfuls of leaves dipped in the water, and when they at last put on their rags again felt like new men. Percy was able to walk back to the spot they had quitted with the assistance only of Jack's arm. The latter, feeling that his breakfast had by no means appeased his hunger, now started for a search through the wood, and presently returned to Percy laden with nuts and berries.

"The nuts are sure to be all right; I expect the berries are too. I have certainly seen some like them in native markets, and I think it will be quite safe to risk it."

The rest of the day was spent in picking nuts and eating them. Then they sat down and waited for the arrival of their friend. He came two hours after nightfall with a wallet stored with provisions, and told them that he had regained the village unobserved. The attack had been repulsed, but with severe loss to the defenders as well as the assailants; two of their guards had been among the killed. The others had made a great clamour over the escape of the prisoners, and had made a close search throughout the village and immediately round it, for they were convinced that their captives had not had the strength to go any distance. He thought, however, that although they had professed the greatest indignation, and had offered many threats as to the vengeance that Government would take upon the village, one of whose inhabitants, at least, must have aided in the evasion of the prisoners, they would not trouble themselves any further in the matter. They had already reaped a rich harvest from the exhibition, and would divide among themselves the share of their late comrades; nor was it at all improbable that if they were to report the matter to the authorities they would themselves get into serious trouble for not having handed over the prisoners immediately after their capture.

For a fortnight the pilot nursed and fed the two midshipmen. He had already provided them with native clothes, so that if by chance any villagers should catch sight of them they would not recognize them as the escaped white men. At the end of that time both the lads had almost recovered from the effects of their sufferings. Jack, indeed, had picked up from the first, but Percy for some days continued so weak and ill that Jack had feared that he was going to have an attack of fever of some kind. His companion's cheery and hopeful chat did as much good for Percy as the nourishing food with which their friend supplied them, and at the end of the fortnight he declared that he felt sufficiently strong to attempt to make his way down to the coast.

The pilot acted as their guide. When they inquired about his wife, he told them carelessly that she would remain with her kinsfolk, and would travel on to Canton and join him there when she found an opportunity. The journey was accomplished at night, by very short stages at first, but by increasing distances as Percy gained strength. During the daytime the lads lay hid in woods or jungles, while their companion went into the village and purchased food. They struck the river many miles above Canton, and the pilot, going down first to a village on its banks, bargained for a boat to take him and two women down to the city.

The lads went on board at night and took their places in the little cabin formed of bamboos and covered with mats in the stern of the boat, and remained thus sheltered not only from the view of people in boats passing up or down the stream, but from the eyes of their own boatmen.

After two days' journey down the river without incident, they arrived off Canton, where the British fleet was still lying while negotiations for peace were being carried on with the authorities at Pekin. Peeping out between the mats, the lads caught sight of the English warships, and, knowing that there was now no danger, they dashed out of the cabin, to the surprise of the native boatmen, and shouted and waved their arms to the distant ships.

In ten minutes they were alongside the *Perseus*, when they were hailed as if restored from the dead. The pilot was very handsomely rewarded by the English authorities for his kindness to the prisoners, and was highly satisfied with the result of his proceedings, which more than doubled the little capital with which he had retired from business. Jack Fothergill and Percy Adcock declare that they have never since eaten chicken without thinking of their Christmas fare on the morning of their escape from the hands of the Chinese pirates.

THE END

www.ingramcontent.com/pod-product-compliance
Lightning Source LLC
Chambersburg PA
CBHW030540180626
46810CB00005B/1952

The Advanced Grabovoi Codes Reference Volume III

Emotional & Identity Calibration

CRP Structural Codes™ System
Tiered • Indexed • Classified Sequences (Domain 02)

James Hutchinson

Copyright © 2026 James Hutchinson

All rights reserved.

No part of this publication may be reproduced, stored, or transmitted in any form or by any means—electronic, mechanical, photocopying, recording, or otherwise—without prior written permission from the publisher, except for brief quotations in reviews.

First paperback edition: 2026